To Redeem a Highland Rogue

Heart of a Scot Book Two

Enhanced Second Edition

COLLETTE CAMERON®

Sweet-to-Spicy Timeless Romance®

Print Edition

Published by Dragonblade Publishing, an imprint of Kathryn Le Veque Novels, Inc

Additional Dragonblade books by Author Collette Cameron

Heart of a Scot Series

To Love a Highland Laird
To Redeem a Highland Rogue
To Seduce a Highland Scoundrel
To Woo a Highland Warrior
To Enchant a Highland Earl
To Defy a Highland Duke
To Marry a Highland Marauder
To Bargain with a Highland Buccaneer

Dedication

For every reader who longs
for their own romantic escape to Scotland.

"I do want to wed ye, lass.
Ye and no other. Ever."

PROLOGUE

Edinburgh, Scotland
May 1699

SHIVERING, HIS ARMS wrapped tightly around his shoulders, Coburn Wallace huddled beneath the broken cart abandoned behind the rickety tenement he and Mum had lived in until three weeks ago. His empty stomach gnawing at his spine, from his damp and dirty hiding place, he watched the wynd for her return as he did every day.

Days and nights of loneliness, hunger, cold, and terrifying fear.

He'd almost been caught filching a roll the day before yesterday, and didn't dare return to the baker he'd been stealing from.

His bonnie mum with her fiery hair and eyes the color of the sky after a storm had always come back in the morning before. Usually with something for him to eat. She'd kiss his head and wrap her thin arms about him, telling him how much she loved him.

"I promise ye, my braw laddie," she'd vow. "We'll be away from here someday soon. To my brother Artair's keep in the Highlands, where the fresh air smells of heather and there's always plenty to eat."

He couldn't remember a time his stomach had been full, or he'd been clean. A time he wasn't afraid, and didn't lay awake at night, a broken knife clutched in his fist, as he listened to the wretched sounds echoing through the thin walls.

"And I can have all the Scotch pies and oat cakes I want?" he asked.

"Aye, my jo," Mum said, pressing her rough palm to his cheek.

"And clootie dumplin's and cock-a-leekie soup and black bun…so many good things." She'd wiped a tear from the corner of her eye with her knuckle. "My brother was right. I never should've left. Never should've trusted yer…"

My da.

Coburn couldn't remember him at all. He'd deserted them before Coburn's second birthday. Lower lip trembling, he sucked it into his mouth and closed his eyes, remembering his sad-eyed, sweet mum.

After mentioning her husband, she'd always summon a falsely cheery smile and ruffle Coburn's hair. "Never mind. Ye'll see, my jo. We'll be away from here soon. I ken Artair will come for us, one day." Her expression would grow desperate, her features gaunt. "Surely, he must. If no' for me, then for ye."

She'd promised that for years.

Uncle Artair never came.

"How will he find us?" Coburn had asked one time.

"I've written him." That was all she would say. Not how often. When the last time was. How he'd know where to look for them.

"Nae! Leave me alone."

Coburn's eyelids popped open at the pitiful cry. He tried to edge farther into the corner, praying the ugly men didn't see him, too. Today, they grasped two little girls by the arms as they dragged them struggling and crying to the ominous looking hack. Four days ago, it had been two boys a bit older than him and another girl.

They weren't the only vermin who preyed on the orphans and street urchins. Covering his ears against the girls' pathetic cries, he squeezed his eyes tight, and pressed his face against his bent knees.

Mum. I'm so scared. Please come home soon.

"I wrote my brother again," Mum had said that last morning, an ugly new bruise on her cheek and a cut on her lower lip. She never answered when he asked her how she came by them. "If anythin' happens to me, ye must stay here so Artair can find ye, Coburn."

Coburn had thrown his arms around her thin waist, hugging her with all of his might. "Nay, Mum. Dinna say that. We'll be together always."

"I hope so, my braw lad." She kissed his forehead. "I hope so."

Paler than usual, she'd crawled into the filthy bed they shared and had fallen into an exhausted sleep without singing to him like she normally did.

The next day, she hadn't returned in the predawn hours. She'd forbidden him to leave their tiny room without her, and made him keep the door locked at all times.

He'd pushed the only chair in the room underneath the tiny, grungy window. Standing upon its cracked seat, the uneven legs wobbling, he watched for her.

Two days later, the landlady turned Coburn out onto the street. The sour-faced, and even fouler smelling wretch, confiscated his and Mum's meager belongings, claiming the rent was late.

"Where are ye, Mum?" he muttered into his knobby knees, tears wetting the torn fabric. "Why did ye leave me alone?"

Chapter One

Outside Edinburgh, Scotland
McCullough's Masquerade Ball
April 1720

ARIEEN'S HEART KNOCKED behind her ribs as she trained her attention across the ballroom. Barely able to breathe, she could scarcely contain her glee. She barely refrained from rubbing her hands together or grinning in triumph.

Och, I have the lying scunner now.

Aye, she did. She good and truly did. And not any too soon, by Odin's gnarly teeth.

Their wedding was scheduled for next week.

Though a domino covered the upper half of his aristocratic face, she easily recognized her loathsome affianced: Fulbright, Viscount Quartermain—every bit as pretentious and full of self-importance as the Englishman's pompous name implied. His lordship also wore a black cape and a tricorn festooned with a ridiculous froth of ostrich feathers.

Ever the charmer—much like the wily serpent in the Garden of Eden—he smiled, dipped his head, and spoke to acquaintances as he ambled along the ballroom's perimeter.

On the other side, about as subtle as a two-headed trow sipping tea in the parlor, Mrs. Jameson, his current love interest, mirrored his movements.

Did they truly think no one noticed their unified, oh-so-casual meandering toward the terrace doors?

After all these months, did *he* think Arieen was such a naïve bam-pot?

Aye. He did.

And that was one of the higher opinions he held of her.

Lord Quartermain would soon learn he'd underestimated her. Anger and exhilaration tussled in her stomach, and an answering wave of anticipation and heat swept over her. She inhaled a soothing breath and slowly, deliberately released the air through her nose.

Steady on, she ordered her galivanting pulse.

Stick to the plan.

Stay calm.

Don't give yourself away.

Catch the cheating cawker in the act.

No one, not even Da, could expect her to marry a lout she caught rutting another woman at a ball.

She slid Morag a sideways look.

Her stepmother tapped her toes to the music while fanning herself. Her advanced pregnancy precluded a need for a costume and, therefore, her handheld mask lay on the empty chair on her other side.

Morag ought to be home, abed, and resting—not here chaperoning her stepdaughter.

Arieen had actually counted on that detail.

She couldn't risk raising Morag's suspicions. If she possessed the tiniest inkling that Arieen plotted something, she'd watch her that much closer and ruin everything. Thank goodness, Arieen's mask and oversized pirate's hat helped shield her eagerness. To succeed with her scheme, she must escape her stepmother's scrutiny for several minutes. Not a task easily managed.

Arieen hadn't told the viscount what she'd be wearing tonight. She *might've* hinted she'd come donned as a nun complete with a crucifix around her neck and a prayer book in hand, if only to enjoy his eyes glazing over with disinterest. As she and her parents had arrived but a few minutes ago, Quartermain hadn't yet noticed her.

Not that it would've made much difference if he had.

In general, after their initial greeting, he ignored her at social gatherings. That didn't mean he disregarded other women in the same brusque manner. No, indeed. The man attracted willing bedmates faster than an open grain sack lured pesky vermin. She alone was the single female he'd eschewed. Probably because of her unfashionable height and dark coloring.

His disdain stung, although 'twas entirely absurd that it did since she couldn't abide him either. Once, she'd overheard him admitting he preferred petite English blondes, not rustic Highland clodhoppers with big feet. There'd been no doubt to whom he referred.

Was it a wonder she couldn't wait to be rid of the dobber?

The crowd parted, and her gaze collided again with that dashing swashbuckler's she'd encountered earlier. He'd brazenly approached when she'd first entered the ballroom. Evidently, he'd thought her alone and an easy mark for his seductive wiles.

Was that the way of all seducers? Bent on wheedling their way into every woman's bed that caught their fancy?

Morag had succinctly curbed his assumption, if that had been his intent.

Breathless, her stepmother had waddled in and promptly snared Arieen's elbow in a harder than necessary grip. Giving the charming fellow a turn-your-attention-elsewhere glower, and her mouth pursed in a sour pucker, she'd whisked Arieen away before he'd introduced himself.

Was he Scots or English?

His burnished hair suggested Scots.

Now, as their gazes meshed again, a lazy grin hitched the buccaneer's mouth—a much too attractive mouth for a man, not that she generally noticed that sort of thing—and he bent into a courtier's exaggerated bow. The bright azure cloth tied about his longish copper hair fell forward, sweeping the floor.

His charms were wasted on Arieen.

Chin lifted, she presented her profile, sending him an unmistakable message. The impertinent, intriguing jackanape. She didn't need nor want the attentions of another womanizer.

The sensation of being stared at raised her nape hairs and, unable to resist another peek, she cut a covert glance in his direction.

A shoulder braced against the door jamb, he unabashedly observed her, his mouth bent in that same gratified grin.

As heat licked Arieen's cheeks, she averted her gaze, only to have another man snag her attention.

His expression, somewhere between disbelief and interest, he regarded her with disturbing keenness. They hadn't been introduced. She was certain of it. Nevertheless, he seemed uncannily familiar and made her oddly uncomfortable.

To ease her nervous tension, she tapped her fingertips on her thigh.

The crowd shifted and blocked the men from her view once more. Just as well. She must focus on the task she'd set for herself. Besides, rakes, *roués*, and rapscallions—men of Quartermain's ilk—were trouble through and through, and didn't hold the least appeal for her.

Then again, neither did serious, long-faced gentlemen.

Or foolish, comedic, featherbrained chaps.

Or scholarly, bookish men.

In short, she hadn't, in her nineteen years, met a single Scot, Highlander, or Englishman who made her pulse patter and her knees go soft.

Bah to the weak knees folderol.

She'd be satisfied to find a man who conversed with her for more than five minutes without ogling other women or his attention repeatedly straying to her bosoms. She wasn't that boring. And what was it with men and breasts? No males of any other species obsessed as much about them.

With a small huff, Arieen dismissed her rambling musings and concentrated on the matter at hand.

Too bad she dared not drag a witness along for what she had planned tonight. Doing so would only strengthen her position.

It wouldn't do, however.

She couldn't very well approach a friend and ask her to help Arieen spy on the bounder she was supposed to wed in five days. Then pop out—*Surprise!*—and announce her presence at a most indelicate moment, as she intended.

Nae. Not done.

But to see Quartermain's expression if she did dare do so…a secret smile arced her lips. That'd be bloody priceless. There'd be no excuses, no hastily contrived fabrications from the viscount this time. She meant to catch him with his breeches down. Literally.

What were a pair of male buttocks and a few moments' awkwardness compared to her freedom?

Another wave of heat suffused her.

Och, perhaps announcing her presence before he was that far along might be a wee bit wiser. She didn't wish to become a voyeur.

Her attention riveted on the objects of her musings.

Hell's fire.

Quartermain and his mistress had almost made it to the doors.

'Twas now or never.

ARMS FOLDED, COBURN Wallace braced a shoulder against the door frame, battling an insane urge to march across the floor and request a dance with the enchanting pirate. He couldn't, of course, without a proper introduction.

Besides being a tremendous breach of protocol, the fire in her chaperone's eyes might incinerate him on the spot, so heated was her perpetual scowl.

Not for the first time, he condemned etiquette and politesse to hell.

Glancing around, he searched for his cousin, Logan Rutherford, clanking about in an ill-fitting suit of armor. Perhaps he could be persuaded to perform the niceties. As Laird of Lockelieth Keep, Logan boasted many more influential connections than Coburn did.

Coburn preferred it that way. Other than the plentiful feminine distractions Edinburgh offered, he also preferred the less chaotic Highland life.

Truthfully, the only reason he was in the city at present was on behest of Logan. His cousin had needed Coburn to make himself scarce while Logan pretended to be him. As Coburn had warned, Logan's plan had backfired and estranged him from his betrothed even further.

That's why Logan clanged and banged about tonight, making a fool of himself in an effort to win Mayra Findlay's affection. Thank God, Coburn was immune to that sort of sentimental drivel.

Look what love had done to Logan, once a sensible man.

Why, not fifteen minutes ago, he'd said, "Just ye wait, Coburn. Yer day may come yet. And if it does, I'll be right there mockin' ye, rubbin' yer nose in yer warmer affections."

Never. Some men weren't meant to wed.

Coburn was one of them.

Aye, far better to be the laird's steward and second-in-command than expected to marry and produce an heir. Neither of which Coburn had any desire or need to do. He'd seen what became of men and women who allowed themselves to fall in love. He prayed Logan and Mayra would be spared the heartache Coburn's mother and even Uncle Artair had endured for love's sake.

Coburn's gut and lips involuntarily tightened. Thinking of his unfortunate mother always caused that reaction. Filling his lungs with a bracing breath, he tossed off his morbid thoughts. Straightening, he surveyed the teeming ballroom.

Honestly, he couldn't point out one couple present who could claim marital bliss. Either they'd married for gain or position, or the occasional fools who'd professed to wed out of mutual devotion, found one spouse—usually both—seeking other bedfellows soon enough.

He permitted a partial gratified smile.

Och, he, on the other hand, had the best of it: No obligation to wed. No bearing the weight and duties of a Highland chief. And the pleasurable, occasional company of a willing lass.

Perhaps his pockets weren't as deep as he'd like at times, and he couldn't lay claim to a single thing of value except his horse, but his belly was always full, he was clean, and he had a warm place to lay his head each night.

Neither of the latter three had been true as a young boy.

He lowered his lashes for the briefest moment against another onslaught of memories.

Och. Enough.

Opening his eyes, his attention once again gravitated to the bewitching siren.

She wasn't the pale, oval-faced blonde with large round eyes and a rosebud mouth popular these past few seasons. No, slate-black winged brows graced her diamond-shaped face above upturned eyes and an oblong chin with the slightest cleft. Her mouth was slightly too wide to be classically bonnie, but her skin gleamed like polished marble.

An irresistible aura surrounded her.

It had beckoned to him from across the room. So much so, that he'd momentarily abandoned his intent to sample his host's superior whisky in the study and had veered in her direction instead.

More fool he.

Nothing could come of pursuing her.

Not only was she guarded like Windsor Castle or the Palace of Westminster with the king in residence, Coburn didn't dally with innocents. This was also his last night here before returning to Lockelieth and resuming his duties as Logan's second-in-command, amongst other things.

Prudence nudged, and giving a resigned sigh, he opted for McCullough's fine whisky rather than beg an introduction and dance with the bewitching wench. Still, he couldn't deny himself another glimpse…

CHAPTER TWO

ARIEEN OPENED HER mouth to ask Morag for permission to visit the retiring room when Douglas McDowell waved.

A delighted grin arcing his mouth, he wended his way toward her and Morag.

Directly behind him, a look of seductive determination on his face, the pirate strode in her direction as well. Surely he didn't intend to ask Arieen for a dance? She couldn't deny the excited flutter in her middle, but *he* was a distraction she didn't need.

She could escape from Douglas with a hastily contrived excuse. Her instincts screamed the buccaneer would be much harder to elude.

If she even wanted to.

Decision made, Arieen acknowledged Douglas' greeting with an exuberant wave and swiftly changed her tactic. "Morag?" she asked.

"Aye?" Morag turned a bored gaze upon her, raking over her pirate's garb. Disapproval sloped her mouth downward. "I dinna understand why yer father permitted ye to dress like a common wench."

That had taken some doing.

Likely, Da had assumed no harm could come of pushing the bounds now that her wedding loomed near.

"I'm a female pirate." Arieen gave a flourishing wave above her head. "A grand dame of the high seas. A swashbuckling wench who knows what she wants. An independent woman in control of her destiny."

Her stomach took another giddy leap.

Or she soon would be.

From beneath her lashes, she cut the swashbuckler a glance. He'd slowed his steps, and then firming his mouth, pivoted and marched the other direction.

Finally. He'd taken her not so subtle hints.

Then why did disappointment sweep her?

"Ye look like a strumpet," Morag huffed, disapproval riddling her countenance. "I canna imagine what his lordship will think."

Och, since his lordship was wont to bugger *hoores* on a regular basis, he would probably think it a grand costume. She didn't dare voice that thought aloud, however.

"I'm sure Mr. McDowell means to ask me for a dance, Morag. I should hate to disappoint our kindly neighbor."

Morag sniffed and pursed her mouth. "Yer father said ye might dance with him. But only once, mind ye. Laird Quartermain is most jealous and possessive of ye."

Bile burned Arieen's throat and nausea tightened her stomach. What a cartload of horse droppings. Most of the time, Quartermain looked right through her. 'Twas her vulgarly large dowry he was enamored of, and he'd never pretended otherwise.

No one had.

Nonetheless, she forced a compliant tone and said, "I didn't think we'd dance more than once."

For the fourth or fifth time since arriving, she absently reached for her fan hanging from her wrist, only to remember she hadn't one to wield. Instead, she grazed the handle of the small dirk sheathed at her waist and winced at the overtight stays torturing her ribs and waist.

Da had no idea she carried a real blade. Two actually. The other was a short sword. The blunderbuss shoved into her belt wasn't loaded though. He also hadn't an inkling she meant to put an end to her unwanted betrothal before evening's end—no matter what it took, short of sticking Quartermain with one of her weapons.

On second thought, if that was what it took…

"Mrs. Flemin'. Miss Flemin'."

Douglas made an elegant leg. Well done for a man his size, truth to tell. An earnest fellow, not one for costumes or fripperies, he'd donned a simple black domino.

"Mr. McDowell," Arieen and Morag murmured in unison.

Sitting taller, Arieen peered over his powdered wig.

Dear Douglas. He'd help her if she asked him.

Except, the instant the viscount had been exposed for the immoral reprobate he was and her troth was called off, Douglas would declare himself once more. He'd done so since she was fifteen, and he'd managed three proposals since she returned from London six months ago. He'd been crushed to learn Da had promised her to that handsome vermin across the room, presently intent upon a dalliance with Mrs. Jameson.

Arieen did love Douglas. Like the older brother she'd never had, and she'd rather lop off a finger or two with her dirk than hurt him again. He'd look at her with those gentle, slightly damp, dark honey-brown eyes and, blinking away the moisture and his disappointment, he would nod his acceptance.

And she'd loathe herself for months and months afterward.

In any event, Da would never agree to a match between them.

True, Douglas owned a nice parcel of land, several head of sheep and cattle, and a not-unimpressive home. His stables boasted fine horseflesh, too. He mightn't have the deepest pockets, but his coffers weren't empty either. Alas, he didn't possess a title, nor was he nobility—two requirements Da insisted upon.

Since Da had married Arieen's former governess six years ago, they'd become obsessed with Arieen making a brilliant match and acquiring a title. Basically, using her generous dowry to buy—*bribe*—a prestigious husband.

She couldn't even argue the arrangement was unusual. Maddening as 'twas, arranged unions, marriages of convenience, even forced unions were as common as mice in oats.

How, though, could Da have promised her to a *Sassenach*?

A prig who'd take her from her beloved Scotland?

How?

Especially that foppish piece of…*shite*?

She allowed a mutinous curve to tip her mouth.

Her tutelage in refinement mightn't have been as successful as Da had hoped. Not nearly as fruitful, truth be known. In fact, she'd been a dismal failure at most everything except learning to speak like a proper Englishwoman, and that singular accomplishment dived south faster than a cannonball in the ocean when she became upset.

Despite the handsome fees Da had paid for Arieen's education, his money hadn't bought her acceptance or respect. For the most part, she'd been treated like an upstart commoner, shunned and belittled for her Scots heritage. But Da needn't ever know that unfortunate fact.

Her nerves bowstrings' taut, she searched the room for her unfaithful betrothed once more.

Arieen curled her hands into fists, so tightly even through her gloves, her nails pressed sharply into her palms.

In accord, Lord Quartermain and Mrs. Jameson casually angled toward the doors at the ballroom's far end.

That's it.

Out ye go.

Find a hidey-hole to roger in.

I'll be along shortly.

Please dinna wait for me to begin yer romp.

Arieen bit her lower lip, smothering the laughter her coarse humor produced.

But how to escape Morag's shrewd regard? She'd have to exploit Douglas, and he didn't deserve to be mistreated in that way.

But neither did Arieen deserve the disrespect and humiliation the viscount and Mrs. Jameson were dealing her.

From behind her mask, Arieen eyed Mrs. Jameson's scandalously revealing Roman goddess toga.

Mayhap the hothouse was their destination.

Mrs. Jameson's virginal white gown—scarlet better suited the woman's reputation—and the brisk April evening didn't allow for a carnal frolic amongst the shrubberies. Although it wouldn't be the first time Lord Quartermain had mated like a randy hare in the bushes.

On multiple occasions, his lordship had returned indoors, slightly out of breath, his striking face *riddy*, and Arieen had spied a bit of leaf or blade of grass in his previously perfectly styled wig. He attributed his breathlessness to a brisk walk in the fresh air.

As for the assorted greenery poking from his curls?

Giving her an indulgent, condescending smile, he'd brushed long, elegant fingers down the sleeve of his purple, or gold, or pink, or whatever other gaudy color he wore that night, and suggested Arieen consider wearing her spectacles more often.

Odious oaf.

She only needed her pince-nez for reading, not for spying foliage adorning his ridiculous wig. Did he think her dafty?

"M...m...may, I have th...this dance, Miss Flemin'?"

Douglas swiped a dab of moisture from his upper lip with his handkerchief. Before he'd returned the monogramed cloth to his coat pocket, more beads appeared.

A horde of unwashed bodies in a too-confined space resulted in a beastly hot and malodorous ballroom. God's teeth, she should've stuffed a fan inside her belt, too. The foul odors wafting about were reason enough to need the accessory.

Laying her palm in Douglas' huge paw of a hand, she stood. "I'd be delighted to join you in a set, Mr. McDowell."

Although they'd been neighbors Arieen's entire life, Morag insisted on formal addresses.

A future viscountess must act the part of a lady at all times, Arieen, her stepmother lectured. Then she'd order Arieen about like a servant.

"Please return Arieen directly to my side when ye've finished, Mr. McDowell."

Morag adjusted her lace fichu. Her bosoms, as well as the rest of her, had grown enormous in recent weeks, and her garments strained at the seams.

Giving Arieen a severe look, she flattened her palms on her grotesquely-mounded belly, a tender smile framing her mouth. She wasted no opportunity to remind Arieen that after three miscarriages, in a matter of weeks, she'd bear Da a child.

No one needed to say Arieen's parents prayed for a boy-child. Neither did anyone have to explain the bairn was also why Morag was eager Arieen wed soon—but only to a peer, mind you.

As improbable as 'twas to conceive, Morag's social aspirations exceeded Da's. Arieen presumed he wanted aristocratic blood to run through his descendants' veins. Morag, on the other hand, craved the social connections and prestige such an arrangement could afford her and the child she carried.

Hence her climbing into the wealthy, aging shipping magnate and spice merchant's bed, and finding herself with child within weeks of becoming Arieen's governess. Da married Morag, but she'd lost that babe three months later.

So she claimed.

An unspoken doubt had always niggled in a secluded corner of Arieen's mind as to whether her former governess had been pregnant at all.

Morag hadn't had an easy time of it with her succeeding pregnancies and openly admitted she feared childbirth. Arieen's mother had died giving birth to a stillborn son nearly fourteen years ago. Though she'd only been five years old, Arieen recalled that awful night and despite Morag's keenness to be rid of her stepdaughter, Arieen worried about her, the bairn, and the birth.

From across the ballroom, Da gave Arieen a *dinna-forget-ye-are-betrothed smile.*

A sad twinge pained her heart. She swept her gaze over the other women present. Each of them was a pawn in one way or another, too, even Morag.

Arieen steered her focus back to her father.

Other than permitting her to attend tonight's ball, he'd never once listened to her pleas. Everything he did served a singular purpose. Stifling a scorching surge of rebellion, she tightened her grip on Douglas' arm.

Eyes questioning, his face creased in concern.

"Remember, come back straightaway," Morag reminded them. She made an exceptionally attentive prison warden.

Douglas slanted his head in agreement. "Aye, Mrs. Flemin'."

Arieen made no such promise.

CHAPTER THREE

If Arieen's plot to catch Quartermain fell through, she meant to switch to her second, more audacious plan, the consequences be cursed.

Could she go through with something that scandalous and compromise herself?

Hopefully, I shan't have to resort to such extremes.

As Douglas led her toward the dance floor, she tried not to appear too obvious, craning her neck to learn if that toff, Lord Quartermain, had made the terrace.

For voicing her dismay at her father's choice of husband, Da had confined her to the house this past month. She'd only seen her betrothed twice in recent weeks, both humiliatingly brief exchanges supposedly to discuss wedding details. Almost immediately, Quartermain had requested a private conference with Da, she suspected to collect promised funds.

Only by pretending to accept her lot and engage in the wedding planning had she managed to convince Da and Morag of her sincerity. She assumed that was why he relented and allowed her to attend tonight after all.

Arieen had finally been presented the chance she'd long awaited and, by jimble, she wasn't going to let it pass.

Da openly admitted he'd married for position when he wed Mother. He'd likely have done so again if Morag hadn't found herself with child. He'd shocked many by doing the decent thing and marrying the beauty, only slightly older than Arieen.

As long as Arieen could recall, he'd been keen on arranging a brilliant match for her. She was confident he wouldn't want a scandal tainting the dynasty he'd methodically built.

Surely, he wouldn't.

He hadn't sent her to live in England for three years and paid a small fortune to have her tutored in etiquette and other essentials in order to mold her into a woman of refinement to then waste the efforts on a philanderer like Quartermain.

Had he?

She paused near an empty bench tucked into a quaint nook and reached for her fan again. Cool leather strips met her searching fingers as they brushed over the handle of the sword sheathed at her hip.

By Odin's toes.

No fan to give credence to her fib of being overheated.

Well, she'd have to improvise. That was all.

She waved her open palm before her face.

"Mr. McDowell—Douglas?"

His eyes rounded and a pleased smile arched his mouth. A nice mouth, but not as impressive as the pirate's.

God, what am I thinkin'?

Certain that red tinged her cheeks, she flapped her hand faster. Thank goodness her flushed face would only lend credence to her lie.

"I'm fare parched from the ungodly heat of this room. Would you mind terribly fetching me something to drink?" She joggled her wrist toward the ornate bench. "Perhaps we can sit here and cool off instead of dancing? I'm certain Morag won't object."

An expression between disappointment and relief washed over his unremarkable features. He also possessed two left feet, making him almost as awful a dancer as she.

Another area in which she'd failed miserably while in England.

"Of c…course, Arieen," he agreed readily. "I'll b…be right

b…back."

The instant he turned away, and the throng swallowed him, she made straight for the nearest doorway, praying neither Da nor Morag would spy her.

If memory served, a library lay farther along, which likewise opened onto the terrace.

She cast a furtive glance over her shoulder.

No one paid her any mind.

As she rushed along the corridor, passing side passage after side passage, the tiniest stab of guilt poked her for deceiving Douglas.

She'd make amends. She would.

Once back in the Highlands, she'd bake black bun and invite him for tea.

"Arieen. When did you arrive? 'Tis been ages since we've seen you."

Swallowing an oath, Arieen plastered a smile on her face as she turned to greet Berget Jonston. Emeline LeClaire accompanied Berget, and delight framed their pretty faces.

Normally, Arieen would be thrilled to encounter her friends.

It had been over a month since she'd seen them, thanks to Da's confinement. But every second that passed meant she might lose her chance to catch Quartermain.

"Och, yer costume is positively charmin', and risqué, too." Emeline, dressed as a shepherdess, complete with a tall staff and a riot of bronze ringlets framing her face, looked down at her peasant skirt. Sighing, she plucked at the fabric. "Aunt insisted I wear *this* travesty."

No one said no to Madame LeClaire, a strictly religious woman and the daughter of a French count.

"'Tis fabulous, indeed, Arieen. Oh, my word you've a sword and a dirk, too." Berget bobbed her head and, as usual, a dark russet curl escaped. Lines of annoyance puckered her forehead as she tried to tuck the unruly tendril beneath her elaborate Egyptian headdress.

"Darlings, forgive me, but I'm in desperate need of the necessary. I think the fish I ate earlier might've been off." Arieen grimaced and pressed a hand to her midriff, managing to subdue a smile at their similarly sympathetic and horrified countenances.

"I'll find you as soon as I am able, and we'll have a nice chat."

After fluttering her fingers, she swung in the other direction without waiting for their responses. She hated her rudeness and dishonesty, but the situation required it.

She *must* catch Quartermain in his indiscretion.

She could not marry him. She simply could not.

God help her if Berget and Emeline came upon Morag and mentioned Arieen wasn't with Douglas. Perhaps she should've taken them into her confidence. She hadn't a doubt they'd cover for her. Especially Berget. A widow at one-and-twenty, she'd been forced into a loveless horror of a marriage at seventeen. She'd understand Arieen's desperation to avoid the same fate.

But Madame LeClaire would punish Emeline severely. More than once she'd locked Emeline in her closet-like chamber without benefit of a candle and fed her nothing but gruel for a week.

Turning part way around, Arieen searched the passageway, and relaxed a fraction.

Excellent.

They'd disappeared into the ballroom.

Her satisfied smile slipped, and her heart tripped over itself.

Och, ballocks and bilge rats.

Douglas stood beyond the entrance, two glasses in his hands as he slowly swiveled in a circle searching for her. He spoke to a man wearing armor much too large for him before the fellow shook his head and clanked away.

Breath held and skirts hiked indecorously high, Arieen ran the last few feet down the corridor. With a cautious glance around, she tested the study's handle. A victorious smile tipped her mouth as the latch gave way, and with another hasty glance down the length of the empty passageway, she edged the door open and slipped inside.

With luck, it would be several minutes before her parents noticed she wasn't dancing and came in search of her. Enough time for her to set her plan in action.

Intent on the drape-covered elongated windows, she scarcely glanced at the hearth's low fire. One hand pressing the short saber of her pirate garb against her hip, she scooted around a marble-topped table.

A moment later, she'd shoved aside the draperies and fumbled with the latch.

"Come on, ye bloody blighter. Open up."

She untied her mask and, after removing it, stuffed it well inside her bodice.

Och, much better.

She squinted in the subdued light. With a soft *click* the lock at last gave way.

Holding her breath again, she edged the panel open and leaned forward, scanning the terrace and lawns beyond. A half-moon faintly illuminated the gardens, walkways, and a burbling fountain topped by a naked Grecian statue.

Did the Greeks never wear clothing?

She pulled back into the shadows as a large kilted man, his features undiscernible from this far away, tramped through the lawns on his way to the house. Once he'd passed, she peeked out again.

A flash of white around the far corner of the house, followed by a seductive giggle and a low groan met her avid scrutiny.

Quartermain and Mrs. Jameson weren't wasting time, nor had the conservatory been their destination.

Staying close to the house, using its shadows to conceal herself, Arieen crept along the veranda. A breeze whisked past, and despite her satin gown's layers, she shivered. Her hackles rose, as did the hair on her arms, almost in a sense of foreboding or as if she were being watched. Pressed to the house's cold brick exterior, she examined the area.

Nothing out of the ordinary met her scrutiny, and her lungs uncramped.

One thing was for certain, she'd make a horrid spy.

She nearly chuckled at the absurd notion.

More primal sounds drifted to her from the shadows, and a blush warmed her face as she turned her attention to the task at hand.

Her plan had seemed feasible when she concocted it. But with the moment actually upon her, she found it rather more disconcerting than she'd imagined to disturb a couple in the act of sexual congress.

Nothing for it.

Once she'd interrupted the viscount's *tête-à-tête*, he would have no choice but to cry off.

This very night she'd be free of the jackal.

Best get to it then.

Shoulders thrown back and head high, she stepped forward. At the same instant, a strong hand roughly clasped her elbow, jerking her forcefully back against a hard-as-brick chest. She and her captor grunted at the impact.

Two ridiculously muscled arms encircled her, holding her captive, as a man clapped one callused hand over her mouth and whispered in her ear.

"Nae, lass, ye'd be interruptin'."

CHAPTER FOUR

COBURN SHOOK HIS head to dislodge the ostrich feather tip attempting to tunnel its way into his left nostril. He tried to subdue the infuriated—*or maybe frightened*?—tempting armful wriggling and twisting, while cursing against his palm.

At least that was what he presumed the outraged muffled threats she spewed were.

"Shh, lass, I mean ye nae harm. Ye were about to intrude upon a private moment."

Biting his hand, she elbowed his ribs and attempted to kick his shins. One boot heel connected with his ankle, and he grunted, his calf radiating in pain.

Hellion.

Her perfume, the merest bit musky, sweet and dark, jasmine and myrtle perhaps, enveloped him. He lowered his nose to her nape and breathed in her heady essence. A woman's scent, sensuous and warm.

Delightfully rounded in all the appropriate places, the top of her head reaching a scant inch past his shoulders, this wasn't a wee, frail lass. He found himself breathing hard as he strained to gently subdue her without hurting her or being pummeled in the process. Another well-placed elbow to his gut knocked the air from his lungs.

"Och, ye wee banshee."

Nae verra wee.

He spun her around until she faced him, her arms trapped between their chests.

"Ye great sod," she grunted, her voice low and quaking. Hands fisted, she beat upon his torso. "Let loose of me. I ken what they're doin'."

He barely avoided the knee she drove toward his groin. The powerful blow connected with his inner thigh instead.

Hell's bells.

She'd damned near rendered him a eunuch. All because he'd taken it upon himself to save her tremendous embarrassment.

The lass strained away, stretching her neck to glimpse beyond the house and exposing the ivory column of her delicate throat.

"Ye're ruinin' everythin'," she hissed, accusation sparking in her eyes. She emphasized her frustration by kelping him in the chin.

"I said let me go! I *must* see them in the act." Low and raspy, her ire-filled voice resonated with desperation.

She liked to watch intercourse, did she? Unusual, for a woman, but not unheard of. Voyeurism wasn't a preference of his.

He'd have sworn the lass was an innocent from the way the enormously pregnant dragon had hauled her away earlier. Before he'd pitched protocol aside and introduced himself, at that.

He chuckled, avoiding another kelp to his chin.

"I'd no' believed a lass as protected as ye appear to be had a taste for peepin'."

"What?" Eyes owlish, her pretty mouth slack, she blinked several times and appeared utterly appalled.

He bit back another intrigued chuckle.

"Nae, 'tis no' like that, ye filthy-minded cull," she denied with a scathing glower.

He gave her his most devilish wink. "If ye say so, lass."

Had her murderous glare been a blade, she'd have gutted him.

Maybe 'twas maidenly curiosity?

Couldn't she simply watch animals then?

He recalled again the comely, but stern-faced woman whose hostile glare had shriveled his ballocks less than an hour ago. Mayhap this lass was guarded fiercely, and animal copulating was a forbidden sight, too.

Soft murmuring echoed from behind the house.

The amorous couple had finished. Mighty swiftly, too.

His beautiful prisoner must've heard their voices as well. Her eyes, the mystical green of Loch Tolhorf after a Highland thunderstorm, and fringed with the same rich ebony as her hair, rounded, then grew glassy.

"Nae," she whispered. "Nae."

She shook her head, and those confounded enormous feathers attacked his face again.

"They canna be done that quickly. They canna." Her half-glance upward only came as high as his chin. "Can they?"

Gut clenching, he tried to swallow against the dry thickness in his throat. An innocent then.

"Aye, lass, they can," he said, his voice dropping an octave.

Shoulders slumped, she sank into him, resting her forehead on his chest and sobbed softly. Her perfume wafted upward again, the trace wholly intoxicating, naughty and nice like her.

'Twasn't his concern but, honestly, she seemed rather too overwrought at having been denied a voyeur's peek. Nonetheless, the need to comfort her overtook him, he cradled her sloping back and quivering shoulders.

A feather tip invaded his nose, and he sneezed. "Damnable hat."

He plucked the tricorn from her head and with a droll grin, tossed it onto a nearby bench.

The cloud of midnight hair he'd admired earlier swirled around her shoulders and down her back. He couldn't help but seize a handful of locks in his fist and raise the strands to his nose. Desire, hot and powerful, sluiced through every pore.

She jerked her chin upward, rage glinting in her eyes.

Taken aback, he loosened his grip a fraction and leaned away, studying her face.

By Odin, she was truly furious.

And absolutely ravishing.

Trembling from outrage or disappointment, she sneered, her stubborn jaw thrust outward mutinously. "Ye've sentenced me to a lifetime of hell, ye interferin' arse. This was my only chance. My *only* chance."

He had an absurd desire to touch his tongue to the cute indentation in her chin.

She closed her eyes, sheer agony etched upon her exquisite features. "Oh, *God,*" she moaned. "The weddin' is next week. I dinna have any more time. What will I do?"

No doubt looking like the thoroughly confused idiot he was at the moment, Coburn shook his head.

"Weddin'?"

She went rigid, her expression contemptuous.

A shudder of…what? Awareness? Lust? Trepidation? Mayhap all three rippled down his spine.

She jerked her adorably clefted chin in the direction of the muted voices. "Yes. My wedding to that philandering, *Sassenach* sot."

In an instant, she transformed from fiery Scot to regal British lady, her speech as refined as an Englishwoman's, though it still held a hint of lilting brogue.

Why hadn't he seen her before? He regularly visited Edinburgh and had been here weeks this time. A finger to his chin, Coburn studied her, then comprehension dawned.

"Ye wanted to catch yer betrothed cheatin' so ye had a reason to call off the union?" Coburn asked.

"Yes," she mumbled through inflexible lips, angrily wiping her cheeks with her fingertips. "If I haven't any voice in whom I marry, I never want to wed."

Poor lass.

Didn't she know her betrothed's behavior was commonplace?

She'd need a much stronger reason for her affianced to beg off than being caught in an indiscretion, especially since he didn't appear the noble sort. Not if he engaged in rogering ladies against houses in the cold night air.

No, her intended seemed more of an opportunistic bugger. Disgust and revulsion for her betrothed vied for supremacy, even as compassion twisted his heart for her.

Her trothed and his lover's voices grew louder, and his captive pirate pinched her full lips together.

"Arieen? Are ye out here?"

A man called into the night from the other side of the terrace.

"Da." The word exploded softly from her lips.

So, her name was Arieen.

It suited her dark elegance.

Panic rounded her eyes, and her chest rose and fell as she gulped frantic little puffs of air. She swept a wild glance first to where the ardent couple were about to emerge before careening behind Coburn to where the other voice had summoned her.

Her obvious desperation triggered his alarm as well. He'd tried to help but feared he'd waded into far more than he'd anticipated. He released her and plowed a hand through his hair, dislodging his scarf. It floated to the ground, puddling at their feet.

She followed the fabric's progress before gradually lifting her gaze to his. Something acute and worrisome flickered behind her eyes, then was gone in a flash.

Expression undecipherable, she shoved her gown off her sloping shoulders. So far off, in truth, he had a lovely glimpse of the ample mounds pushed high by her stays. A red, black, and gold mask lay snuggled between the pearly flesh, and only with supreme effort did he keep from grinning and plucking it from its lucky nest.

She glanced at her bare shoulders and, lips flattened into a straight ribbon, yanked one side down farther—clear to her elbow—exposing her stays and the lacy chemise underneath.

What was she about? Perchance she wasn't a complete innocent, after all.

"Arieen? Arieen Gillian Kinna Flemin'. If ye're out here, answer me this instant, ye insolent lass." Her father's voice rang with impatient anger. "Why didna ye watch the lass closer, Morag?"

"Dinna ye dare blame me, Robert. The ungrateful wretch was supposed to be dancin' with Douglas McDowell. I told ye allowin' her one last ball was a mistake. Ye should've kept her locked in her chamber until she exchanged vows with Viscount Quartermain."

A viscount? Och now.

One hand on his hip, Coburn angled a brow at her. 'Twasn't every day a lass scorned an alliance with a lord, even if he was a bloody *Sassenach* sot.

Wait a buggering minute.

He cut a brief glance over his shoulder. Had the woman said they'd locked Arieen in her chamber? She'd been held prisoner in her own home? Confined by her parents and was being forced to marry a man she clearly despised?

Pity bathed him, replaced a moment later by contemptuous anger toward a couple he'd never met. His premonition screamed a warning, and he swung his focus back to Arieen. Distracted by her plight, he'd delayed too long.

She'd slid a dirk from her belt and pressed its cutting edge to his ribs.

Coburn could've easily wrested the knife from the fascinating lass, but perverse curiosity demanded he know what she intended.

"I dinna believe ye'll skewer me for denyin' ye yer peepshow, lass."

"Really? I have nothing to lose, thanks to you, Mister…?" She laughed, a brittle, hollow sound. "I don't even know the name of the churl who ruined my life."

The breeze blew a few raven tendrils across her face, but she remained stock still, her blade angled.

How experienced was she with the dirk?

Was he fool enough to find out?

"'Tis Coburn Wallace, and ye're Arieen Flemin'. Any relation to Robert Flemin'?"

She gave a single, terse nod. "His daughter."

Scorn's acidic taste filled his mouth. Offspring of one of the richest, most unethical cits in Scotland. Did Miss Arieen Fleming take after her foul sire? Nothing Coburn had witnessed suggested she did, but then women could be most convincing and conniving if the need arose.

He looped a stubborn fluttery strand of hair behind her ear—*aye, even softer than the tendril appeared*—then gave in to the impulse to trail his forefinger along her jaw.

To his utter astonishment, she raised onto her toes and touched her mouth to his. First tentatively, but with increasing fervor he never would've suspected she possessed. Mayhap she *had* watched copulations or, at the very least, had kissed a few lads.

Except her kisses were clumsy and lacked the finesse of a woman practiced in the art.

"Kiss me back," she demanded, her tone throaty.

"Lass, I dinna…"

The blade pricked sharp and sure.

Mayhap he *had* underestimated her.

"Kiss me. Now," she ordered, her mouth against his.

She wanted revenge against her viscount.

He could give her that much.

Damn him for a fool, Coburn cupped her head with one hand and splayed his other against the hollow of her back, forcing her chest to his. He plundered her mouth like the buccaneer he was attired as, and she answered like the wanton wench her costume suggested.

Lust exploded and, for a long moment, 'twas just the two of them, breaths and tongues intermingling.

She went soft and pliable in his embrace, her free hand clasping his back, and he arched her neck for deeper access to her sweet mouth.

"Arieen? Is that you? What the bloody hell goes on here?"

Chapter Five

QUARTERMAIN'S HAUGHTY AFFRONT doused Arieen's unanticipated ardor, but inflamed her ire all the more. Struggling to compose herself, she settled back onto her heels as she stepped away from Coburn Wallace.

She expected him to hightail it but, instead, his expression amused, he folded his arms and cocked his head. His hair swished to the side, brushing his shoulders. He had lovely hair for a man.

And that beautiful mouth…

Lord, she'd kissed those lips and enjoyed it.

Exhaling, she sheathed her dirk while sweeping an admiring glance over his sculpted torso. A thin scarlet ribbon glinted above his ribs. Ribs that had rippled with solid muscles while he cocooned her in his equally impressive strong arms.

Hound's teeth.

She'd actually cut him.

A complete accident, but that didn't lessen her remorse.

Aghast, she raised an apologetic gaze. "I've hurt you," she whispered. "I truly didn't intend to. Forgive me, please." Though she spoke of the cut, she also meant for using him in such a callous way.

That wonderful mouth of his quirked into a playful grin as he examined his side.

"Dinna fash yerself, lass. 'Tis only a scratch. I've had worse."

When she'd tossed all common sense to the rubbish pile and demanded he kiss her, she'd been intent on one thing: being caught in a compromising position. Beyond forcing Quartermain to beg off, she hadn't considered the consequences, and that had been utterly, unpardonably stupid.

Self-loathing throttled through her veins. She'd been unfair to Mr. Wallace, a total stranger.

The immediate, inflaming desire when they'd kissed had shaken her to her core and thrown her off course. Her wits yet flitted about like inebriated butterflies.

Wouldn't you know it. A *braw mon* who finally made her bones melt and caused her pulse to flutter. A Highlander, too, smelling of the outdoors and his own unique manly scent. And everything about the situation was wrong, wrong, wrong.

He'd never forgive her for exploiting him.

However, if her scheme had worked…

After righting her bodice, she faced her betrothed straight on.

Quartermain advanced, stalking forward, his bearing incensed and menacing. Masked and cloaked in black, he appeared sinister. Almost evil.

A jolt of apprehension skittered across her shoulders. This side of him she'd not seen before. Honestly, it didn't surprise as much as unnerve.

"I expect an answer, Arieen. You are my affianced. Why were you kissing this…?" He flicked his fingers disdainfully at Mr. Wallace. "Highland *scum*?"

Upper lip curled, he spat the word as if spewing offal from his mouth.

What would he do if she told him it was none of his business?

But it was.

One of Mr. Wallace's copper brows shied high on his forehead, and a rigid jaw and steely glint in his eyes replaced his jovial countenance. "I'd watch my words, if I were ye, ye prancin' *Sassenach* bampot."

"Arieen, answer me," Seething, his nostrils flared, for an instant, she thought he might strike her.

How dare Lord Quartermain be offended?

She'd but kissed a man. He'd had *relations* with Mrs. Jameson out in the open where anyone could've stumbled upon them.

Arieen lifted her head in bold defiance. "I'll explain myself, my lord, when you enlighten me as to why you were shagging Mrs. Jameson in full view of anyone who might've passed by."

"No sense trying to explain a woman's needs to a child." Mrs. Jameson, rather than looking appropriately abashed, appeared entertained. She had the audacity to wink at Arieen. "The risk of discovery makes it all the more thrilling, my dear. You're a lucky girl. Fulbright is very *rigorous* in his attentions."

She didna mean…?

A superior smirk lit Mrs. Jameson's eyes.

Aye, she did, the hoore.

She and Quartermain deserved each other, the degenerates.

Mrs. Jameson cast the men a coy glance and slanted her kiss-swollen lips upward.

In invitation?

Was the woman never satisfied?

Plastering a syrupy smile on her face, Arieen stared pointedly at Mrs. Jameson's attire. "You've dirt smudges on the back of your—whatever that filmy thing is you're wearing. My, I wonder how you'll explain those away? Oh, and there's a bit of moss or perhaps spider web in your hair, just here."

Arieen touched the side of her head, indicating where the stringy substance dangled on Mrs. Jameson's curls.

Mr. Wallace chuckled as Mrs. Jameson scowled and brushed at her intricately styled hair, while straining to see the blotches marring the back of her gown.

Shoulders bunched, Quartermain lowered his chin, reminding Arieen of a cranky Highland bull. He flexed his fingers, as if barely restraining himself from grabbing Arieen and shaking her.

She wasn't certain he wouldn't have, save for Mr. Wallace's and Mrs. Jameson's presence.

"No betrothed of mine acts like a common harlot. You've much to learn about my expectations, Arieen. I promise you'll swiftly modify your behavior once we're wed. I've no qualms about keeping you locked in your chamber until you learn how to act."

She reared back, retreating a couple of stumbling paces, her pulse beating a ragged rhythm.

He couldn't be serious.

"I am not marrying you, my lord. My father may covet your title, but I most assuredly do not." She shoved her hair over one shoulder. "You've engaged in one indiscretion after another since the onset of our troth, and I'm positive my father shan't want that dishonor associated with his name."

Doubt niggled.

Would Da care?

Oh, God.

So sick to her stomach was she all of a sudden, she might have truly eaten bad fish.

What if she'd miscalculated?

What if her disgrace was all for naught?

What if Da *didn't* care about a scandal?

Nonetheless, desperate to sever the agreement, she pressed her point. "Our betrothal is at an end, my lord."

Quartermain's harsh, mocking laughter sent chills streaking from her neck to her toes.

"You're more ignorant than I'd imagined. How do you suppose I met your father, you stupid chit?" He leaned in, a cruel smile twisting his lips. "We met at a brothel. Very exclusive, of course. Only the most discriminate of courtesans, but a whorehouse nonetheless."

A distressed sound, half-gasp, half-involuntary objection escaped Arieen, and she swallowed the bile burning her throat. Shame condemning her, she couldn't stand to look at Mr. Wallace.

Mrs. Jameson, on the other hand, appeared unaffected by the viscount's revelation.

"That's where your father first approached me about a union between us," Quartermain said. "He kept offering me larger and larger settlements to take you off his hands. He only cares about the brat in your stepmother's belly. Hopes it's a boy he can leave his legacy to. Told me so himself."

Arieen shook her head, sorrow crushing her chest. "I don't believe you. That's not true."

Except, even before he married Morag, Da hadn't been a doting father, and he'd become less so these past few years.

Maybe...

Maybe he hadn't cared he mightn't ever see her again if Quartermain did, indeed, lock her away as he'd vowed. A shudder born of fear and betrayal juddered across her shoulders, and she gulped against the lump blocking her throat.

"Ye've said enough, Quartermain." Disgust laced Mr. Wallace's words, and his posture had become intimidating as well.

What she wouldn't give for him to knuckle the arrogant smile from Quartermain's face. Except striking a member of the peerage had serious consequences. Och, she could punch him in the nose.

"It's Lord Quartermain or my lord, you gutter riffraff." All aristocratic arrogance, his lordship raked a caustic gaze over Mr. Wallace.

Mr. Wallace's slow, deprecating scrutiny of the pompous British peer raised him another notch in her esteem. "I generally dinna fawn over horses' arses."

"Swine." The viscount presented his back to Mr. Wallace then seized Arieen's wrist in a bruising grasp.

"Your esteemed sire isn't the saint he pretends. Though I cannot say I blame him for tupping trollops, given his fish-harpy of a wife. Tricked him into marrying her, he said. Claimed she was increasing when she wasn't, the enormous cow."

Her father and Morag rounded the house's corner, and no doubt existed they heard his lordship's every word.

Morag clutched Da's arm, her full face ashen.

Da puffed out his scrawny chest, all self-righteous indignation. "How dare ye speak such codswallop about me and my wife, Quartermain?"

Lord Quartermain released Arieen's wrist, and she rubbed the reddened flesh.

"Don't pretend offense. You're not sure the whelp she now carries is yours." He gave a mocking wink. "But you're willing to overlook that *minor* detail if the babe's a boy."

"Nae," Morag choked and stabbed Da with a wounded glare. "Nae."

Mrs. Jameson sniggered behind her hand, and Mr. Wallace made a harsh, disapproving sound in his throat.

The viscount, the evil craven, casually flipped his cloak over one shoulder before proceeding to pull his gloves from his coat pocket.

Da's pallor now matched his wife's. He opened and closed his mouth twice as he wiped his broad forehead with the back of his hand.

"My dear, please let me explain." He reached for Morag's arm, but she swatted his hand away.

Swaying unsteadily, she snapped, "Dinna touch me."

Arieen rushed to her side and wrapped an arm around Morag's thick waist.

"Come. Sit." She urged her stepmother to the bench, nudging her discarded hat aside to make room.

Releasing a gusty sigh, Morag sat heavily upon the stone, both hands cradling her swollen belly. Eyes shut, she propped her head against the rough bricks and sagged into herself.

She didn't look at all well.

A crowd had gathered behind them, including the massive Highlander wearing a kilt Arieen had seen earlier. Berget, Emeline, and Douglas hovered on the throng's outer edge, their countenances taut with confusion.

Summoning his dignity with obvious effort, Arieen's father focused on Mrs. Jameson and Mr. Wallace for the first time. Brows tugged close in censure, his attention slid over Mrs. Jameson before coming to rest on Mr. Wallace.

"Who are ye, sir?"

Did that mean Da already knew Mrs. Jameson and what her association with the viscount was? And it hadn't mattered? He still intended Arieen should wed his lordship?

Treachery, sharp and jagged, stabbed her.

"Coburn Wallace." Mr. Wallace offered nothing more, but his gaze sought the kilted giant's.

Friends? Acquaintances? Enemies?

None of that signified at the moment.

"Da, let's find someplace private to talk. Morag doesn't look well. The study is around the corner—"

Suspicion narrowed her father's eyes to slits, and he swung his accusing gaze between Arieen and Mr. Wallace.

"Exactly what are ye doin' out here with my daughter, Mr. Wallace? Are ye aware she's betrothed to Lord Quartermain?"

"Oh, they were enjoying a delightfully naughty assignation," Mrs. Jameson offered with a falsely helpful upward sweep of her mouth.

Sounded more like what the tailwag had engaged in with the viscount.

Or wanted to do with Mr. Wallace.

"A last dalliance before she weds, perhaps?" Mrs. Jameson thrust home another barbed jab.

A few of the women huffed, not necessarily in reproach, but in excitement at the succulent tidbit, and another buzz of whispers echoed from those gathered.

Shock, disbelief, accusation, and finally resignation played across Douglas' face before he turned his back and disappeared into the night.

Despair engulfed Arieen, and she dropped her chin to her chest to hide her tears. She'd tarnished more than her reputation tonight. She'd lost a dear friend—a cost she foolishly hadn't counted.

Mouth cinched tight, a distressed sound escaped Morag.

Holding her icy hand, Arieen pleaded, "Da, please. Let's go inside. Morag needs to lie down."

True bafflement knitted her father's wiry brow. Head cocked, his little eyes unblinking, he peered upward, insect-like at Mr. Wallace. "A tryst? But that's no' possible." Bewildered, he faced Arieen. "Ye've no' left the house for a month. How do ye ken him?"

"I don't." She sent Mr. Wallace a desperate look. "I mean, we met a few minutes ago…"

Och, that sounded bad.

Really bad.

A cunning look entered Quartermain's eyes as he lazily assessed the others gawking at the tragedy playing out before them. "Do you mean to tell me I caught you in a passionate embrace, your bosom practically exposed, with a man you'd never met before?"

Humiliation sluiced Arieen, the truth of his accusations rubbing her raw. Dash her impulsiveness. She'd managed to immerse herself into this mess. She'd just have to figure a way out.

He threw his head back and laughed. "Oh, this is too providential to be true." After a few more hearty guffaws, he brought his humor under control. "I cannot possibly take such an immoral creature to wife."

Oh, praise God. Thank ye. Thank ye.

"My lineage must remain unblemished," he said, "and such a woman casts a sinful shadow on the viscountcy and my honor."

"Never mind your rutting and philandering and how those have tarnished your already dingy honor," Arieen snapped. She ought to be appalled she'd spoken so rudely to a peer, but she wasn't in the least.

Rage sharpened the viscount's features. "Have a care you don't push me too far."

His carefully modulated voice sent chills down her arms, and she curled her toes in her boots against the instinctive urge to retreat.

Fear mingled with her relief.

He'd publicly rejected her. Her goal had been accomplished—but she worried it might be at a far greater price than she'd anticipated.

Arieen tucked her arm behind Morag, intent on helping her stand.

"I do, of course, expect to receive the dowry in full per our agreement, Fleming." His lordship adjusted his mask upward on the right side.

Partially hunched over Morag, Arieen twisted to stare at him fully. Jaw slack, she steered her gaze to her father.

Eyes bugging from his head, he opened and closed his mouth several times. His face as red as a skelped arse, she feared he might be in the midst of an apoplectic fit.

Why hadn't she considered this?

Och, how could she have?

She didn't know the exact terms of the marriage settlement. There must've been a clause regarding breaking the troth, and Quartermain had seized upon it like a starving dog thrown a bone by the butcher.

Hypocritical toad.

"After all, *I* didn't breach the contract, Fleming," Lord Quartermain said with a haughty upward angling of his jaw. "Your daughter did."

Chapter Six

"That's a lie." Arieen jerked upright. "You were out here with her." She stabbed her pointer finger at Mrs. Jameson, affecting an innocent mien.

"Miss Fleming, I cannot countenance what you infer," Mrs. Jameson said. "Are you casting aspersions on *my* reputation? When his lordship and I clearly saw you, in *scandaleux déshabille*?"

Now the uppity bint tossed her French around?

Jaw tense and frustration thrumming through her veins, Arieen pressed onward. "Mr. Wallace and I heard you in the act, and it's not the first time you've been indiscreet either, my lord."

Och, how it galled to have to defer to his title when he was no gentleman.

"Truth be known, I've lost count of the number of times," Arieen said.

"Ah, but did you actually *see* anything?" Quartermain's tight smile betrayed his motives, his utter aristocratic arrogance. "For I certainly saw *you*."

Arms folded, Arieen directed an impatient scowl at him. She wasn't playing his game. Ironically, she had the witness she'd desired. Yet apparently, when it came to men of power, even with proof, they escaped justice. But a commoner such as she? Well, she was guilty until proven innocent.

"Mightn't you have been mistaken, Arieen?" Quartermain asked, condescending derision dripping from each word. "After all, you were a distance away and obviously otherwise engaged."

How could he become impossibly smugger? Jaw clenched, she fought an overwhelming urge to tell him to go bugger himself. Or flatten his perfect nose with her fist.

The planes of his face hard, Mr. Wallace shook his head, and rubbed his jaw.

"Nae. I ken well the sound of barnyard matin'. The squawks, and gruntin', and..." He arched a russet eyebrow at Mrs. Jameson. "Most especially the swine-like squeals."

More titters and chuckles filled the air.

"Well. I never..." Mrs. Jameson finally took offense, and after leveling him a withering glare, flounced away, her nose pointed high.

Faces rapt, the other onlookers remained rooted in place. Berget and Emeline exchanged anxious glances and clasped hands. Arieen foolishly hadn't considered how her ruination would affect her friendships.

Stupid, stupid lass.

Every door might be closed to her now. Including Berget's, as she had returned to her parents' house when her husband died, and his eldest son had booted her to the curb.

Lord Quartermain pulled on his other glove. "I'll come around tomorrow morning, Fleming, and we'll discuss the settlement details. The courts take breach of contract seriously. And I'm happy to say, they tend to look more favorably on those of noble birth."

His oily smile curdled the contents of Arieen's stomach.

"I'd say this worked out very well, indeed," he said to no one in particular. "My purse will be filled, and I don't have to shackle myself to that cloddish Highland wench, after all."

He delivered the last with such contempt, Arieen fully understood what she'd barely escaped. The viscount loathed her as much as she despised him. Given his cruel streak, God only knew what he'd have done to her if they'd actually wed.

Looking well-pleased, he strode away.

Arieen whipped around to face her father and was gratified to see Mr. Wallace's glare burning dual holes into Quartermain's back.

Morag moaned, clutching at her stomach.

"Morag?" Trepidation suffused Arieen. First a flush of heat fired behind her breastbone, spreading to her limbs, then icy cold chilled her heart, dampening her underarms.

Dear God, the babe wasn't due for another month.

Da rushed to the bench and dropped to one knee. "Is it our wee bairn, my love?"

"Dinna ye, *my love* me," Morag spat, perspiration beading on her brow. "Tellin' his lordship ye dinna ken if the bairn is yers." Her voice turned plaintive. "How could ye, Robbie?"

Mouth pulled downward and shoulders slumped in shame, he hung his head. His wig slipped forward, and he impatiently shoved it farther up his forehead. "He lied. I swear."

Had he? Arieen no longer knew what to believe.

"I didna say all the things his lairdship said I did. I was pished, though. Ye ken how men are when they've been quaffin' a dram or two." At her stony stare, his demeanor became wheedling. "I was desperate for him to accept Arieen and wed her before the bairn came, just as ye'd asked."

A penetrating chill seeped into the marrow of Arieen's bones, but not from dread. Da's public admission caused her heart to cramp, an unrelenting punishing vise of betrayal. This wasn't the time to dwell on her hurt though. Morag was in labor.

"Da, we need to get Morag home and send for the midwife." Arieen moved to slip her arm around Morag's shoulders, but her stepmother shoved her away.

"This is yer fault," Morag said, her face contorted in pain, her eyes squinted and accusing. She licked her lips, her wild gaze darting here and there. "If ye hadna lied, this upset wouldna have happened. I may lose another bairn," she moaned. "I shall never forgive ye, Arieen. Never."

"Nae, my darlin' lass." Da awkwardly patted her shoulder. "We'll get ye home. Everythin' will be fine. Ye'll see."

The glower her father directed Arieen might as well have been a rusty sword hurled to her middle, such did it impale and gut her.

"My wee bairn. My wee bairn." Rolling her head from side to side, Morag groaned again.

Arieen staggered to her feet. Tamping down fear and bile, as guilt brutally accused her, she turned to the crowd. "Someone, please have our carriage brought around to the entrance at once." Thank God their house was only a few blocks away. "And can someone else go for Howdie Smellie? She lives on Cumberland Lane."

She ran her damp palms down her skirt, surprised to find they shook. *She'd* never forgive herself if something happened to the baby.

Mr. Wallace motioned to the tall man and, at once, the Scot strode forward. "Graeme, go for the midwife. Take her directly to the Flemin' residence. Also, ask a footman to have their carriage readied immediately." Mr. Wallace briefly studied Morag's puckered face. "Ask Broden McGregor to fetch Doctor Ballingall as well.

Howdie Smellie wouldn't like that. Nevertheless, Arieen couldn't deny her relief another who knew something of childbirth would also attend Morag.

"Ye canna miss McGregor," Mr. Wallace said. "He's struttin' about dressed as an Arabian sheik."

"Aye, Coburn, I saw McGregor earlier." Thumbs linked inside the wide leather belt at his waist, Graeme kept one eye on Morag. "But ye came with me. How will ye get home?"

Mr. Wallace combed a big hand through his bright hair. "Dinna fash yerself. I can always hire a hackney. Now go. Please."

"Aye, then." Graeme hurried away, and a couple of guests followed.

To help, or were they eager to share the scandal they'd witnessed?

Mr. Wallace directed his attention back to Morag and Arieen. "How can I be of assistance?"

He seemed to speak to Arieen, rather than Morag or Da.

"Ye've done enough already, Wallace." Da sneered.

"Come, Morag." A hand on either elbow, Da helped her stand. "Everythin' will be all right. Ye'll see. We need to get ye home and tucked into bed. The bairn will be right as warm porridge in the morn."

"Let me help you to the carriage." Once more, Arieen tried to add her support on Morag's other side.

"Nae," Morag hissed through clenched teeth as another contraction wracked her. "I dinna want ye anywhere near me. Ye've always been jealous of me and my bairns. Always wanted yer da to yerself."

"That's not true," Arieen whispered. She'd never resented Morag or the children she'd carried.

Such animosity contorted Morag's face, Arieen dropped her arm to her side, and could only look on helplessly.

Mr. Wallace edged to her side, his presence warm and welcoming. He spoke low into Arieen's ear. "Leave her be, lass. Women in the throes of labor say all manner of ugly things they dinna mean. She'll no' even remember her temper afterward."

Casting him a swift glance, she encountered his encouraging smile. She tried to summon her composure and tilt her lips upward in acknowledgement, but failed. "How do you know?"

He quirked a brow. "I've been nearby on several occasions when a bairn made its way into the world."

Now that was just plain peculiar. As much as he'd raised her curiosity, Arieen's focus remained on her stepmother.

She understood Morag's fear, and perhaps her accusations were justified about the early labor's onset. After all, what did Arieen know of childbirth? Nonetheless, the hostility directed toward her stunned.

Throat aching with unshed tears, she sidestepped away and glanced to the crowd. How had it grown this large without her noticing? Guests regarded her with pity or sympathy, others with accusation and condemnation, and a few seemed amused or enjoyed the spectacle.

The whole time, Mr. Wallace remained by her side, almost in a protective manner.

Da searched the crowd and motioned to a pair of matrons. "Please assist my wife to our carriage."

The women hurried forward, all empathy and caring, one to either side of Morag. No doubt their husbands owed Da money.

"Robbie?" Morag grimaced as another contraction overcame her.

"Never fear, my dear. I'll be along in a trice, and we'll make sure ye're settled comfortably at home. I need a wee word with Arieen first."

Before he finished speaking, he seized Arieen's elbow, then roughly guided her to the end of the terrace.

"Och, Da." She winced at the crushing grip. "You're hurting me."

Trying to disengage her arm, she cast Morag an anxious glance.

Hunched over, a ghastly shade of gray, her stepmother had made the entrance with the other women's help.

Hands on his hips, and his face etched into hard planes of concern, Mr. Wallace regarded Arieen. He opened his mouth, as if he intended to interfere or object, but she shook her head.

He had no right, and Da was already in a fine fettle. He practically dragged her along and didn't release her until they rounded the corner.

Somewhere out here is where the viscount had dallied with Mrs. Jameson.

Her stomach churned anew at the ugly truth.

She rubbed her sore arm. For certain, she'd have a bruise. He'd never laid a hand on her before. It must have been fright for his child and wife that had Da this overwrought.

"Da, cannot whatever 'tis you want to say wait until we get home and make sure Morag and the bairn are safe?"

"Nae, it canna wait."

The way he glared at her, as if he could barely stand to look upon her, sent a shudder tiptoeing across her shoulders.

He'd become a stranger in an instant.

"Da?"

The earlier premonition returned with renewed force.

"I've waited nineteen years to say this." He jerked his lopsided wig back into place. "Even Morag disna ken the truth. I've cared for ye, been kind to ye, treated ye like my own flesh."

The increasing breeze blew more strands across her face. Arieen impatiently brushed them away. "I don't understand. I am yours."

The evening had grown cold, and she wrapped her arms around her shoulders.

"Nae, ye are no'. I gave ye my name, but ye are no' mine. Why do ye think yer mother, a noblewoman, would marry the likes of me? She was carryin' ye, the seed of her blue-blooded lover, when we wed. But she died birthin' my son. *My son!*" He jabbed his chest with his forefinger. "All these years I've patiently waited to have my own child."

Arieen's mind reeled in denial as the puzzle pieces settled into place. Robert Fleming hadn't wanted her around.

It all made sense now. How he'd always been too busy for her. How she'd been left in the Highlands with nurses and governesses when he'd spent most of his time in Edinburgh. Why he'd sent her away for three years, and she'd not been allowed one visit. How she'd been summoned home, already promised to Lord Quartermain, then locked in her chamber when she'd said she'd rather marry Widow Gebbie's ancient, one-eyed boar.

It had been no accident Robert had promised her to a man who'd take her from Scotland.

She clamped her jaw to stop her teeth from chattering, not from cold, but from shocked hurt.

"Morag has taken my seed to her womb four times. Three of those, I've grieved mightily when another bairn died." He swallowed audibly and shook his head, glaring at her with such loathing, tears burned behind Arieen's eyelids. "The child she carries means more to me than ye ever have," he said. "I owed ye nothin', yet I tried to find ye a position and a title."

Pain twisted her heart with each harsh word. His determination to see her titled was more for his and Morag's benefit than hers, but now she understood it wasn't just lust for position. They truly wanted to be rid of her.

"And this is how ye repay me, Arieen?" he said, lifting a hand as if to strike her. "Ye're like yer loose-moraled mother."

Such disgust and contempt shone in his eyes, she gasped and retreated a few swift steps.

He dared accuse her of wickedness and besmirch her mother when he'd been frequenting brothels? How she so longed to be brave enough to speak her thoughts, but she'd pushed him too far already.

"Ye could've been a viscountess, but ye and yer pride, yer high opinion of yerself. Ye tossed yer only chance for a decent match away. Do ye think anyone will have ye now?" Gesturing wildly toward the house, he spat upon the ground. "I'm good and done with ye, Arieen."

A sob ripped from her throat, and a single scalding tear trailed down her cheek. She fisted her hands tight against her sides to keep the fragile amount of control and pride she had left intact.

"I'm goin' to have to honor the settlement terms which will cost me a bloody fortune, and I dinna benefit from it at all. Ye've shamed me and my name with yer slatternly behavior," he ranted on. "And now..." His hostile glare scraped over her, leaving her as raw and tender as if he'd taken a dull razor to her. "And now, I may lose *another* child."

His pain ripped through her, stark and ragged.

His voice broke and, chin quivering, he gulped several times in an attempt to rein in his emotions. "I'm no' a young mon. This may be my last chance to father a child. A son."

Dashing at another tear, she touched his arm, needing to make amends. She wasn't remorseful that she'd tried to avoid marriage to Quartermain, but with everything in her, she regretted causing the early onset of Morag's labor.

"I am truly distressed—" She couldn't call him Da now. "I never meant harm to come to the bairn or Morag. I didn't think—"

"Nae. Ye didna."

Jerking away, he turned his back. He might have lifted a drawbridge, so deep and wide was the chasm between them. So impenetrable and fortified, the wall he'd erected.

"Please." She extended a hand in supplication.

He mightn't have been the most doting or affectionate father, but she'd loved him. Morag, too. They were all the family that Arieen had ever known.

Except for servants and the time spent in London, she'd been isolated most of her life. She'd tried to be brave. To not complain. To find something to appreciate. But never, *never*, had she felt as unwanted and utterly lonely as she did in this moment. A dreary, cold, gray shroud enveloped her, and she wrapped her arms around her shoulders.

"What would you have me do?" she asked through the vise clamping her throat.

He gave a disinterested lift of one shoulder. "Ye are nae longer my concern, and ye are no' welcome under my roof. Send word where ye are stayin', and I'll have yer clothin' and personal belongin's delivered there. 'Tis more than ye deserve."

"But…" She swallowed acrid, salty tears, real despair battering the walls of her chest.

She had no family that she knew of. There'd never been contact with her mother's relations. Neither had she friends able to take her in for a time. Or a position and means of earning a living.

Surely, he wouldn't be that cruel.

"Canna ye send me back to the Highlands?" She hated the desperation in her voice, yet she beseeched him. "Ye'd never have to see me there."

"Nae. Morag wants to raise the bairn—if he lives—away from the city. I've already sent word to have the house readied for our arrival.".

"Where shall I go?" she asked in a small voice, hating how pathetic and desperate she sounded. But she *was* desperate.

He spared her a scornful look over his shoulder; the mask he'd worn all these years ripped away from grief and anger.

"I honestly dinna care, Arieen. Consider yerself disowned from this moment forward."

CHAPTER SEVEN

AFTER MRS. FLEMING had departed and Fleming had hauled his astounded daughter out of sight, Coburn shooed the others inside. The curious guests had witnessed enough dramatics to keep them entertained and the rumor mill buzzing for weeks to come.

His focus gravitated to the terrace's shadowy far end.

What could've been so urgent that Fleming sent his distressed wife to their carriage alone?

If Coburn's wife were in labor, he'd have seen to her care first.

A wry chuckle escaped him. That was the first time he'd ever considered being a father. For reasons he couldn't identify, the notion didn't appall him as the idea generally did.

He didn't know if he could be a good father. What example had he had? His own sire had deserted him and his mother when he was a toddler. Coburn didn't remember him at all, and Uncle Artair had been a manipulative cull who'd betrothed his six-year-old son for gain. The men who lived in the slums, the home of Coburn's early years, weren't exactly model parents either.

The question that begged answering just now was, why did he linger on this frigid terrace?

He wasn't waiting for Miss Fleming, he admonished himself.

Nae.

Not at all.

He was simply making sure no harm came to her.

Hadn't Fleming already proved he was a scunner when it came to his daughter?

Besides, Coburn acknowledged, he was partially responsible for this situation. He didn't have to kiss her. He could've walked away. Refused her enticing invitation.

And heather didna grow in the Highlands.

Why he cared about the well-being of a woman he'd only just met mystified him more than it should. Spending the evening worrying about a stranger was not how he'd envisioned his last night in Edinburgh. No, more romantic pursuits had topped the list. Perhaps his cousin Logan's gentlemanliness and nobleness *was* rubbing off on him.

Hound's teeth. What a horrid concept for an admitted Highland rogue.

A bonnie Egyptian queen—was she Berget Jonston?—and a serious-faced shepherdess he wasn't acquainted with loitered outside the ballroom's entrance. They kept casting worried glances toward where Arieen had disappeared with her father. At last, after exchanging a few whispers, they slipped into the ballroom.

His scarf dangling from one hand, the wind whipping the ends about his legs, Coburn, too, sought the house's warmth.

Likely, Arieen and her father had re-entered the mansion through a different doorway. No sooner had the thought crossed his mind than Fleming rounded the terrace corner.

He stamped toward Coburn, his shoes clacking nosily on the flag stones. His face berry-red and his spine rigid, the diminutive man fisted his hands and snarled, "She's ruined. Nae decent mon will have her now. And ye are no' remorseful, are ye, ye scurrilous swine?"

Was her ruination the cause of his anger, or was his fury due to the viscount having fled the cage?

With another disgusted upward curl of his lip, Fleming stomped away.

Coburn had a few choice words he'd like to have said, none of which were an apology. Not to Fleming, in any event.

Expecting Arieen to follow on her father's heels, he stepped back onto the veranda to apologize for his part in this disaster.

She was nowhere in sight.

Mouth pulled into a harsh line, he slid Fleming's retreating back another glance.

Why wasn't his daughter with him?

How was she supposed to travel home after he accompanied his wife? Surely arrangements had been made. Although, a cur who imprisoned his daughter mightn't worry himself overly much about how she was to find transportation.

'Twasn't Coburn's nature to entangle himself in private matters, so his concern baffled him all the more.

"What are ye doin' lurkin' by the door, Wallace?" Liam MacKay grinned, the movement stretching the scar lashing his right cheek taut. Liam shook his shaggy black, silver-threaded head. His costume, a Roman gladiator, fit the burly Highlander and flattered his muscled calves. "Normally, ye'd be flirtin' with a dozen lasses, decidin' which should warm yer bed tonight."

"Ye exaggerate." Not by much, truth be told. Unfamiliar chagrin scratched Coburn's pride.

Wearing an exasperating smirk, Liam rubbed his bountiful beard. He ought to trim the unkempt bush. His wife had despised it, which, Coburn would bet his favorite whisky, was why Liam kept it.

"Graeme said ye created yerself in a wee bit of a predicament."

Coburn merely quirked a brow.

"Were ye actually caught kissin' Flemin's daughter? I didna think ye fool enough to dally with respectable lasses." Liam crossed his ankles and leaned a shoulder against the doorframe, his sword clanking against his shield. "Is it true? Flemin' insists ye marry the lass?"

Coburn's gaze snapped back to his friend.

Leave it to the gossips to fabricate horsesh—jobby. He re-tied the scarf around his head. "Nae such thing, and she kissed me, nae the other way around."

Initially, anyway. It had been a moving kiss, too, and he could yet taste the sweetness if he ran his tongue across his lips.

"I'm nae about to be trapped into marriage over a stolen kiss." He peered past Liam.

Where in Hades was Arieen?

Inside now? He scanned the ballroom, then veered his gaze toward the far doors. Maybe the study, where he ought to be indulging in a dram of some of the finest spirits in Scotland? He shifted his focus to another entrance. Could she be in the ladies' retiring room?

It wouldn't surprise him if she'd escaped to there to regroup after the debacle outside.

"I didna expect to see ye here," he murmured, never stopping his search for Arieen. Liam loathed assemblies such as these. Probably because he met his dead wife at a similar event, and such gatherings always stirred unpleasant memories.

"Och, well..." He scratched his neck, working his gray-eyed gaze over the throng, until they lit upon a chestnut-haired beauty dressed like shield-maiden and chatting animatedly with a Roman or Greek goddess and a...*pear*?

Someone ought to have done that poor woman a favor and advised her against the green atrocity.

"It's Kendra's birthday. Mother insisted I play escort," Liam offered by way of an explanation, and he adored his sister.

Arieen had yet to appear and something Coburn refused to acknowledge as alarm prickled his nape. "Will ye please excuse me, Liam?"

There was no way in hell he was explaining what he intended. He'd never hear the end of it if he admitted he went in search of Arieen. By God, he couldn't explain to himself why he did.

Liam dipped his chin, and with an awkward pat on Coburn shoulder advised, "Be careful. A mon like Flemin' canna be trusted. He didna get filthy rich by bein' a kind-hearted gent, and I've found with wenches fruit disna fall far from the tree. The lass mightna be better than her sire, and her kissin' ye might be part of a calculated plan."

If he wasn't genuinely sincere, Coburn would've laughed. Liam spoke from personal experience, and aside from his mother and sister, he trusted no other women in Scotland.

"She refused a viscount," Coburn said. "Why would she try to entrap me? Ye ken full well, as Logan's cousin and second-in-command, I dinna own my own house. I've little to offer a wench, if I ever entertained the idea of marryin', which I dinna." *God help me if I ever become that dafty.* "Nae, she said she didna want to marry at all, and I believe her."

Actually, she'd said if she couldn't have a husband of her own choosing she didn't want to wed.

"Watch yerself," Liam advise, his visage warrior serious. "Lasses have a way of trappin' a mon before he kens what's happened. Regrets and recriminations make for poor bedmates."

He ought to know.

Fierce creases marring his once handsome face, Liam slipped a flask from inside his costume and, raising it in a silent salute, strode out into the chilly night.

Coburn scanned the crowd once more, his gaze hitching on Arieen gliding into the ballroom's other side.

Ridiculous relief flooded him.

She must've used the study entrance after all.

Several people presented their backs as she passed, but shoulders squared and head held high, she swept past them. Regal as a Highland chieftainess, she made directly for the Egyptian and the shepherdess huddled in a corner.

From where he stood, he recognized the relief on her friends' faces as she approached.

Arieen spoke briefly, then floated away, as gracefully as she'd entered, heading once more to the passageway leading to the study. She paused and glanced over her shoulder, her ravaged gaze snaring his.

The air left his lungs in a mighty whoosh, much like a punch to his gut.

Several people bent their heads near and whispered as she walked away, and a handful of men assessed her in a lewd manner that made Coburn want to plant his fist in their faces.

The gossips had wasted no time rendering judgement.

He was as guilty as she of being imprudent, but he'd get sly pats on the back and winks from the men—likely invitations from the more brazen of the women as well, while Arieen faced ostracism.

After furtive glances around, their heads bent near, her friends followed her.

A rickle-a-bones, sharp-faced dame abruptly excused herself from a conversation, and after signaling to Lady Stewart, the pair met by the doorway. Ah, the Egyptian *was* the widow, Mrs. Jonston, and Lady Stewart, her gentle, rotund mother. The women exchanged a few covert words amid several fretful glances down the corridor. Lady Stewart gave a reluctant nod, and they casually linked arms, strolling after the younger women.

What went on here?

Coming to a sudden decision, Coburn escaped onto the terrace once more. Except for a couple clinging to each other by the fountain, no one else was about. Lengthening his stride until he was practically running, he soon stood outside the study.

Wouldn't Logan raise a mocking brow at his behavior?

Feeling like a thief, he cracked open the door and looked inside. A sedate fire burned in the grate and two double-tapered candelabras flickered atop the glossy wood mantel, but the chamber was empty. He'd started to turn away when the outer handle rattled. He'd barely enough time to slip behind the heavy draperies before feminine footsteps echoed inside.

A female made a *tsking* noise.

"Did I forget to shut the door?" Arieen asked, her voice oddly hoarse. With swift steps, she crossed the room and pulled the outside door closed. "After this horrid evenin', 'tis nae wonder I'm a wee befuddled."

Did she talk to herself often?

The trait was rather endearing.

Why didn't he reveal himself instead of cowering behind the window coverings like a naughty school boy?

A soft rap echoed across the room before the rustling of skirts and more feminine feet pattered inside.

"Arieen, you've been crying, and your father has left without you," one woman said.

Coburn edged a couple of inches to his right to where the two panels met and peeked between the folds. He'd been reduced to skulking about like the street urchin he'd once been.

He told himself he hid away to spare Arieen more humiliation, but the truth wasn't as noble. He couldn't leave without knowing she was all right. The guilt would plague him endlessly. No saint for certain, he couldn't abandon her, though what he might do to aid her he couldn't fathom.

As he'd said to MacKay, he didn't have his own home, nor had he deep pockets. He could offer her neither a position nor funds.

Revealing himself would be much more awkward and difficult to explain, in any event.

"What did yer father say to ye?" the other woman asked.

"That's what I need to speak with Berget about." Arieen turned desolate green eyes to them. The fierce, confident woman who'd struggled in his arms had been replaced by a stricken one. "Berget, I…"

Arieen cleared her throat, obviously humiliated and uncomfortable.

"What is it Arieen?" Mrs. Jonston's kind smile didn't bely her concerned expression. "You know I'd do anything within my power to help you."

Arieen curved her mouth while twisting her mass of hair into a long rope. "I find myself in an impossible and most humbling circumstance. Might I stay with you for a few days until I am able to find a position and permanent lodgings?"

Coburn stiffened and must've made a sound, because Arieen flashed a puzzled glance in his direction.

What the hell had happened?

'Twas no small matter for a woman to find employment, particularly one of gentle breeding. One whose reputation he'd helped tarnish. She couldn't very well become a barmaid or a governess. Few—frightfully few—respectable choices remained.

"Arieen, what has happened?" The shepherdess voiced his thoughts as she touched Arieen's arm.

Arieen dropped her chin to her chest and released a long sigh. Features strained, she tossed her hair over her shoulder and raised her head.

"The short of it is, Emeline, I'm disgraced and have been disowned. Robert Fleming isn't my father as I've believed and no longer feels the need to bear the burden of my care."

Her voice cracked on the last word, and tears brightened her eyes.

"Oh, Arieen. How utterly awful," Mrs. Jonston said, as she and Emeline embraced her.

The door burst open, and all three women started and exchanged troubled glances as they separated.

The two matrons swished in, and the skinny one with a face like a horse's hind end demanded in heavily accented French, "Why are you cloistered in here, Emeline?"

"I'm having a private conversation with my friend, Aunt Jeneva.

Hence, the shut door." The shepherdess pushed her hideous bonnet off her forehead.

Coburn couldn't suppress a grin at her spirited retort.

The aunt elevated her nose. "*Non*. After tonight's dramatics, you are not permitted to associate with Miss Fleming. *Zut*, you are the granddaughter of a count. Your reputation will suffer."

"Aunt. Ye forget yerself." Emeline thumped the floor with her staff. "Arieen is one of my dearest friends and will remain so."

"*Non,* if you wish to continue to live with *moi*." The aunt's pointy chin jerked a couple of inches higher.

What was with these people threatening to turn their relatives out?

"As I have nae wish for my friends to witness me at my worst, we will finish this discussion privately." Clearly peeved at her domineering relative, Emeline pressed her lips together.

Her aunt's triumphant expression slipped a notch.

"Berget, your father wishes to depart." Lady Stewart avoided looking directly at Arieen.

At only half-past ten?

No, Lady Stewart was taking the coward's way out and fleeing.

Her smile sympathetic, but firm, she extended her palm toward Berget. "Come along, dear. You know your father doesn't like to be kept waiting. We have something important to discuss with you."

Mrs. Johnston went very still, her eyes slightly narrowed as she stared at her mother for a very long moment. Seeming to rouse herself, she said, "Whatever it is can surely wait." Linking her elbow with Arieen's, Berget ignored her mother's hand. "Arieen is coming home with us."

Well done ye, Mrs. Jonston.

Arieen's friends' loyalty did her credit.

Sighing, Lady Stewart dropped her plump hand to her side, where she fiddled with her fan's handle. She glanced at Arieen for a second before her guilty gaze scooted away. "I fear she cannot, my dear. It won't do. We've already endured so much scandal, and your prospects..."

Her voice trailed off at Mrs. Jonston's affronted expression and harsh, inarticulate objection.

Coburn recalled there'd been chatter when Mrs. Jonston's husband died, but he couldn't remember what exactly. Unlike several of the ponces prancing about the ballroom, when in Edinburgh, he didn't sit in upper salons, sipping tea, and begging for an earful of the latest tattle.

"Scandal, if you will recall, Mother, that was *not* of my making." Pulling her spine straight, Mrs. Jonston stared her mother down. "Arieen is my friend, and she needs me. This is what friends and family do. They help each other when no one else will."

More than a little recrimination in those words.

Expression contrite, Lady Stewart shook her head, causing the feather on her mask to bob like a fat goose's tail feathers.

Make that a fat *running* goose's tail feathers.

"I regret you find yourself in a difficult situation, Miss Fleming. I truly do," Lady Stewart said, giving Arieen a transparent look of pity. "However, this very afternoon, my husband met with your father regarding an important business venture. Lord Stewart would be most upset if the offer were...withdrawn."

Business venture or a loan?

Her regard switched to her daughter and a steely—or mayhap desperate—note seeped into her tone. "It's *imperative* 'tis not, Berget."

Loan then.

Was Stewart, like many of the peerage, in debt up to his noble forehead and on the cusp of ruin? And Lady Stewart was far too accustomed to her luxuries to let something as frivolous as common decency stand in the way of maintaining her privileged way of life.

Coburn eyed Mrs. Jonston.

Hadn't her father offered her to her husband as a tantalizing prize, much the same way as Fleming had offered Arieen? Devil take it, why couldn't he remember the particulars?

"I understand, Lady Stewart." Arieen said. "I'd not want my presence to cause you and Lord Stewart angst."

Mrs. Jonston snorted her disagreement, and Arieen offered a brave, if tremulous smile.

Coburn wanted to both shout his admiration for her pluck and sweep her into his arms and assure her all would be set right someway.

He didn't know how yet.

Perhaps Logan might be able to find her a position. Not easily done since she'd been disgraced. Pure idiocy that a single kiss could compromise a young woman.

"I shall not yield on this, Mother." Mrs. Jonston patted Arieen's arm looped through hers, smiling, perhaps a shade over-brightly at her friend. "Arieen, you will stay with us. For tonight, at least."

"That's kind, Berget, but what happens tomorrow?" Arieen asked, her voice the merest shred of a sound.

"Precisely," Lady Stewart agreed crisply.

Before he could think the impulse through or concoct all sorts of logical reasons why what he was about to do was insane, impractical, and plain dafty, Coburn stepped from behind the draperies, causing a collective gasp, widening of eyes, and fluttering of hands.

"Ye'll marry me."

CHAPTER EIGHT

AMID CREAKS AND groans, the hired hack swiftly rounded a gloomy corner. Stifling a gasp, Arieen clutched at her seat. This miserable—smelly—equipage was a far cry from the well-sprung coach she'd grown accustomed to.

Once certain she wasn't going to tumble onto the floor, she relaxed her grip.

"My answer is still no, Mr. Wallace."

Coburn didn't respond right away.

She'd learned one thing about him tonight other than that he was gallant. He listened and carefully considered his replies.

"I appreciate the noble gesture. I truly do, but we are strangers," she said. "We might be"—*most probably were*—"wholly unsuitable for each other. I know less about you than I do Quartermain."

Except, she'd discovered Coburn Wallace kissed divinely. The viscount, on the other hand, had never offered as much as a peck on her cheek. He'd also never have considered rescuing a compromised woman by suggesting they marry, even if the idea was barely this side of dafty.

For whatever illogical reason, Arieen trusted Coburn.

That explained why, at this late hour and despite the impropriety, she found herself in a rocking vehicle reeking of yeast, rank cheese, and God only knew what else.

Maybe 'twas because he'd championed her in front of everyone that she'd agreed to accompany him. Or perhaps, her plight was so pitiable and desperate that she hadn't anything else to lose by going with him to see whatever he was positive would change her mind.

It wouldn't, of course.

She'd have to be off her head to marry him, but that left her in a conundrum of monumental proportions.

The offer to stay at Berget's tonight remained open. Berget had made that perfectly clear before nearly dragging her gaping and sputtering mother from the study.

Arieen intended to accept the one night's hospitality, though it only delayed the inevitable. Perchance, if they put their heads together, she and Berget could concoct a reasonable plan before tomorrow. More likely, however, no ready solution would be available.

Renewed panic zipped along Arieen's spine and, rubbing her hands over her elbows, she shuddered. She'd jumped straight from the boiling pot into the hot coals. Had she known it would come to this, would she have finagled this hard to have the wedding called off?

Aye. She would have. At least now, she could anticipate a change in her circumstances. Someday. If God and several saints smiled upon her. Marriage to the viscount would've stripped her of the possibility.

Better a morsel of hope than none at all.

"I think it's time to turn around, Mr. Wallace. I've already inconvenienced the Stewarts, and their generosity was not freely given but commandeered by Berget, as you no doubt heard."

Arms folded, Coburn towed his attention from the lane and slanted a skeptical brow.

She thought he did anyway.

Unlike the vehicles she was accustomed to, the cab had no interior lamps.

"Ye agreed to see what I mean to show ye, lass, before ye made a decision."

Reluctantly and imprudently, she had.

Arieen had managed to maintain her composure until her curious friends and their mothers had filed from the room. Before Coburn's appearance, Lady Stewart and Madame LeClaire couldn't wait to leave the study, but once he'd popped out from behind the draperies, their pace had slowed to such a degree, a snail might've whisked past them.

Neither Berget nor Emeline were wont to wag their tongues. Unfortunately, the same couldn't be said of their mothers. News of this imprudent jaunt, as well as Coburn's impromptu proposal, had likely swept through the assembly at McCullough's swifter than fire through a hay field in late summer.

In fact, he'd used that argument in his attempt to sway her to his position and accept his impulsive, pity-driven, impossible offer for her hand.

His reasoning hadn't swayed her.

She'd not add entrapping Coburn Wallace into marriage to her list of impetuous idiocies this evening. Except, the truth of it was, she hadn't been impulsive. She'd planned to disgrace herself if it would force Quartermain to call off their union.

Her guilt lay in not considering what harm and inconvenience her actions would cause the man who aided—willingly or naïvely—in compromising her. True, she'd no way of knowing Robert Fleming wasn't her father, or that her actions would set into motion a series of ill-fated events she had no control over.

Nevertheless, she'd politely listened to Coburn's convincing rationale, how he was his cousin's second-in-command at Lockelieth Keep and could provide her a humble but comfortable life, for another fifteen minutes before shaking her head.

As they careened around another corner, she lifted a hand, pointing her forefinger beyond the grimy window.

"You mean to show me Edinburgh's seedier side, gambling my fears will persuade me where your reasoning could not. Yes? The filth and decay? The streetwalkers and pickpockets? The drunkards and beggars?"

She closed her eyes for a moment against their hardened, defeated, street-wise features.

"It's not the first time I've seen those wretches, Mr. Wallace, nor pitied their lot." True, but not this close or in this particular section of Edinburgh. "But my answer is the same. I shan't marry you."

Arieen never *ever* considered she'd be facing the same predicament as the unfortunates outside. She mightn't have been coddled or doted upon, but to Robert Fleming's credit, she'd never wanted for anything—save affection—until this moment.

Now destitute, she admitted to being utterly terrified about her future.

Inhaling a shuddery breath, she tried to formulate a shred of a plan.

She wasn't wearing jewelry she could pawn, although, she might get a few coins from selling the sword, blunderbuss, and dirk.

Searching for a solution, she absently watched the rubbish-littered wynds pass by.

Where could she find employment?

Of more import, in the meanwhile, who would take her in? Edinburgh was notoriously overcrowded, housing was scarce, and she hadn't many connections she could approach about a position or a place to live.

'Twas possible—probable—word of her fall from grace might make it impossible to find work here. Perhaps she should look in London? How could she possibly travel there without money?

What was fast becoming familiar dread sent hopelessness throttling up her throat.

She drew her focus to the brawny man sprawled on the seat across from her. Even in the midst of this crisis, merely glancing at him made her stomach flop. Ruggedly handsome, dangerously charming, and possessing a devastating smile, she wasn't immune to him, rapscallion or not.

Och, 'twasn't that Coburn's offer didn't tempt—didn't provide an answer to her dire quandary. It did both. She was honest enough to acknowledge he'd stirred a passion in her she hadn't known she possessed. But to marry a complete stranger?

Which fate was worse?

The streets? Or him?

At first glance, the streets, obviously. Nevertheless, each choice had her balancing on a precipice's perilous edge.

A few hours ago, she'd only faced an unwanted marriage. Now homeless, without means, and her heart shattered by the only father she'd ever known, her future loomed abysmal.

How could Da—Robert—have harbored so much animosity toward me, and I never kent?

It would be a long while before that wound healed.

Her musings migrated to Morag and the bairn. How were they? How could she find out how they fared? Concern for them still weighed heavily upon her.

"Nae, that's no' what I want ye to see, Arieen. Only a wee bit farther." Coburn's denial pulled her from her reverie.

He returned his contemplation to the tenement slums all around them.

A few minutes later, the carriage shuddered to a stop. Peeking from the window, Arieen meshed her lips together as two rats dashed across the road. Not only did she have no idea where she was, she'd never seen such blatant poverty.

Coburn climbed out and, after handing her down, tossed a coin to the jarvey. "Wait for us. We shallna be long."

The driver gave a grudging nod as he hunched further into his coat's raised collar. "Dinna dawdle. My missus disna like it when I stays out late."

"Ye'll be well-compensated," Coburn said, "and I'm sure yer missus willna mind the extra coin."

Arieen pressed the back of her hand to her nose. "The air is positively fetid. What's that horrid smell?"

"Raw waste, rubbish, offal, dead rodents." His bearing alert and watchful, Coburn searched the road. "Ye eventually get used to the stench."

Coburn took her dirk and tucked it into his waistband. "I ken how to use this better than ye, and we may have need of it."

She gave a slight, trepid nod, and he cupped her elbow.

"Keep yer head down, and dinna speak to anyone," he said under his breath.

Wasn't this a bit extreme to make his point?

He pressed his fingertips into her arm. "Do ye understand, lass?"

"Aye."

An eerie atmosphere hovered in the air, and fear heightened her awareness. Mouth dry, the muscles in her shoulders and back so tight they ached, she licked her lower lip. How did people live like this? Constantly afraid?

"Watch yer step," he softly cautioned, nimbly stepping over a dead rat.

From beneath her lashes, she scrutinized their surroundings. Irregularly-shaped, coal-blackened buildings several stories high surrounded them. Gutters on either side of the wynd overflowed with all manner of foulness. Though 'twas past eleven of the clock, young children and toddlers peeked at them from the tenements' grimy windows and shadowy doorways.

Speaking low, he led her down a narrow alley. "Many of these urchins are on their own. Likely, their mothers were prostitutes who died from disease, abuse, or were murdered. Or they abandoned them."

She jerked her head up, searching his face in horrified disbelief. "How could they?"

"Desperation causes people to do the unthinkable." Alert, his tension apparent in the tight grip on her arm, he continually scanned their surroundings. A few feet farther along, he motioned to two boys huddled beneath a cart. "They sleep wherever they can find a bit of protection from the elements, and they frequently go days without eatin'."

"Poor darlings." She glanced at him to find him observing her, his expression inscrutable. "Can nothing be done?"

He rolled a shoulder. "The Church and a few other charities sponsored by wealthy patrons help."

A girl, not more than eight years old, wearing a filthy tattered gown and sporting a greenish-yellow bruise on her cheek ventured forth. Two smaller lasses, holding hands and huddled together, warily followed her with their haunted gazes.

"Please, sir." The girl held out a grimy palm. "Can ye spare a coin? My sisters be hungry."

Coburn dug in his pocket and pulled a small coin bag out. He gave her one. Other children scrambled from their hidey-holes, begging for money.

Face grim, he parceled out all he had.

Another shudder raked across Arieen's shoulders, from raw emotion and cold. How did these ragamuffins survive the winter months? Why wasn't more being done to lessen their suffering?

In the half-light, she examined the waifs' smudged, tired faces. Faces too old and defeated for their small forms. If Robert hadn't married her mother, she might've been one of these urchins. Bittersweet gratitude stabbed her for what she'd been spared, and she hugged her shoulders.

Several guttersnipes yet jockeyed to get close to Coburn, begging for money.

"I dinna have anymore. I'm sorry." He held the bag upside down and shook it.

The children's disappointed cries shredded Arieen's heart, as she and Coburn turned to leave.

His bearing guarded, he guided her toward the hack. "If they are no' already, those lasses—and aye, the lads, too—will be sellin' their bodies for a scrap of bread."

"Dear God," she choked. Her boot tip caught on an uneven cobble, and she stumbled. The tears blurring her eyes might be to blame for her clumsiness.

He tightened his grip and steadied her. "Careful."

She stared over her shoulder from whence they'd come. "It's awful. And wrong. And unfair. And I feel completely and utterly helpless."

As they emerged onto the main road, she stifled a dismayed cry.

The hack was gone. How were they to get to their destination now?

Walk Edinburgh's most treacherous roads this time of night? Aye, likely their only option since Coburn had given the urchins his last coin.

Grasping her shoulders, he pivoted her to face him. His expression intense and unyielding, he searched her eyes.

"If ye dinna marry me, ye'll find yerself like their mothers, Arieen." He made a subtle gesture to a harlot engaged in an intimate act against a shoddy building. "Like her."

Arieen dropped her gaze, humiliated for the poor woman. "I..." Sickening realization swamped her, and she closed her eyes against the unholy images his words conjured.

"Ye'll be set upon. Violated. Beaten. Abused hundreds of times." He gave her a gentle shake. "Look at me."

Reluctance weighting her eyelids, she raised them, staring straight into his eyes, glittering with raw emotion.

"Maybe ye think ye can avoid that life, or mayhap endure it"—*nae, I canna*—"but what if ye have bairns?" He jerked his strong jaw in the direction they'd come.

Her attention snapped to the dingy alley.

She instinctively closed her eyes and cradled her empty womb in a protective gesture. God above, he was right. In her current circumstances, she mightn't be able to do much to aid these precious children, but she would not knowingly inflict this impoverished life on a child of her own.

"How can ye condemn yer children to such a fate, Arieen?"

CHAPTER NINE

"I WAS ONE of those children," Coburn said, "and I wouldna wish that life on my worst enemy."

He remembered the terror as if it had only been last week. The aching cold and gnawing hunger clawing at his belly. The perverted debauchers trying to bribe him into going with them. He'd never forget running to escape the sods when he'd refused. Or witnessing the abduction of his friends. Or…later, seeing them beaten and broken from the violations they'd been subjected to.

If they returned to the streets at all.

The ebony crescent of Arieen's lashes slowly lifted, and he read the hopeless resignation in her eyes. Her gaze tormented, she captured her lower lip between her teeth.

A drunkard, holding a whisky bottle and singing off-key, shambled in their direction.

Only a fool lingered in the slums, and although Coburn carried her dirk, they risked robbery or worse by remaining. They were outsiders, and from the not-so-covert looks being sliced toward them, others had noticed.

A scrawny cat darted across the road, a limp mouse clamped in its mouth. Probably taking the rodent to feed her kittens.

"Come, we must move along. We're drawin' attention." He took Arieen's elbow and setting a brisk pace, led her away. Logan's residence was under two miles from here. Not a horrid jaunt in the dead of night, but not a meandering stroll either.

He wouldn't curse the jarvey for leaving. Coburn had nothing left to pay him with, in any event. He simply hadn't been able to refuse the children what money he'd carried. Besides, it might do Arieen good to experience a few minutes more of Edinburgh's unsavory neighborhoods. To see the ugly reality her life could become.

She matched his stride, her long hair swishing across the gentle slope of her bum, their boots clicking on the cobblestones.

"How did you escape that life, Coburn?"

Did she hope she could, if it came to that?

Not unless someone helped her. And right now, she didn't have anyone except him.

"My uncle, Logan's father, rescued me. Uncle Artair wasn't the noblest of men, but when my mother—his sister—died and left me a homeless orphan, he found me and took me to Lockelieth. I dinna ken how he kent but, one day, a few weeks after she didna return home, he showed up. Logan, too. I'd never met them before, but Logan looked a great deal like me, and we kent we had to be related."

Coburn's mother had been a whore at the end. He'd seen and heard things no child should ever witness. That was how he knew about childbirth. The tenement walls were paper thin.

He eyed Arieen sideways. "I've seen the verra worst humankind can do to each other, and though I dinna ken ye, I'd spare ye that misery."

He may not have caused her situation, but he'd certainly contributed to her difficulty, and he'd marry her to spare her the fate of his mother. Even if it meant relinquishing a secret, impossible dream. At one time, before Logan's return from abroad, Coburn had considered leaving Lockelieth and taking to the sea. He wanted to see the world, and a poor man had few options available to do so.

If he married Arieen, he'd never be able to pursue that dream, for he'd not abandon his wife or the children they might produce. Neither would he leave them a burden for Logan to care for. He couldn't offer her much, merely respectability and a simple life in the Highlands.

He slid her a covert glance. Forehead furrowed and gaze lowered, she appeared deep in thought as they tramped along. He took a huge gamble, of course.

After all, she was—at least had been—the pampered daughter of one of the wealthiest men in Scotland. Chances were, she'd be miserable.

Better unhappy and safe than a pathetic *hoore* destined to die young.

Coburn was neither rich nor titled, but his position as Laird Rutherford's second-in-command was secure. She'd never go hungry, want for basic necessities, or have a hand raised against her. That was more than countless women could claim, including nobility.

True, years of neglect by Logan's father meant the keep needed restoration, but Lockelieth was the only home Coburn had known. Arieen on the other hand, was accustomed to a more comfortable existence, and she'd undoubtedly find the castle lacking.

He hadn't missed her grimace of distaste when she'd settled onto the hackney's seat, but to her credit, she hadn't complained. Surely life at a medieval keep, despite its rustic trappings, drafty chambers, and occasional—*frequent*—leaks was preferable to the poverty and depravation she'd just seen.

They walked in silence for several minutes, gradually leaving the shabbier portions of Edinburgh behind as they descended the Royal Mile.

"Coburn." Brow knitted, she gave him a considering look as they passed a man pushing an empty cart. "How did you and your mother find yourselves on Edinburgh's streets?"

"I honestly dinna ken or remember the details." He shook his head and scratched his neck. "Uncle Artair wouldna speak of it, except to say my mother had eloped. The details went with him to his grave."

"Families like to keep their unsavory secrets hidden," she said.

No small truth there.

"What say ye, Arieen? Will ye marry me? I leave for Lockelieth in the morn."

He'd been away for weeks already.

As they marched along, she pressed two fingertips against the bridge of her nose. "I don't know. I don't know you, Coburn." She waved a hand toward him. "Isn't there another option? I don't want to marry a stranger, and you cannot desire it any more than I."

"Och, I'm no' altogether keen on the notion either, lass. But nae, I can offer ye naught else that's respectable." A wave of irritation swept him at her continued reluctance. He'd never planned on marrying, let alone rushing into a union with a woman he'd met but hours ago.

A lass with the sweetest kisses I've ever tasted.

He'd not beg her, by Odin's bones.

Arieen was free to choose her own destiny.

He drew her to a halt before the steps leading up to St. Giles Cathedral. "If ye're no' willin', I understand. Tell me where ye want to go, and I'll take ye there. The Stewarts?"

Lord and Lady Stewart lived on the outskirts of Edinburgh. He'd be waking Logan and asking for a few coins after all. 'Twas too far to walk, and he wasn't riding double with that alluring siren. Arieen hadn't stopped shivering the past five minutes, and she wasn't dressed for a nighttime ride, in any event.

A scowl pulled Coburn's lips taut. His cousin would ask questions. Lots of annoying, prying questions. And he'd either laugh until he cried at Coburn's predicament, or now that he'd finally won Mayra's heart, lecture Coburn on his foolishness.

Both notions settled on him like a black, dank cloud, and he found himself impatient for Arieen's decision.

Idiot, he admonished himself.

Had he seriously thought a woman of her background would have the likes of him? Even if she was without other recourse? He should feel relief, not this…nameless, annoying whatever-it-was. Not disappointment exactly—that implied he felt affection for her. And Coburn never permitted sentimental attachments. He loved his lasses, left them smiling and sated, but his emotions weren't engaged beyond fondness for the fairer sex as a whole.

Head tipped back, three lines creasing her forehead, Arieen examined the church's impressive architecture.

A pigeon cooed softly, likely snuggled in a cozy nest with its mate somewhere in the crown steeple. Coburn had anticipated spending the night similarly nestled instead of freezing his ballocks off trying to convince a disinclined lass to wed him.

"Could I not go with you to Lockelieth?" she asked, her focus trained on the cathedral.

Coburn had considered taking her with him, but Logan wouldn't approve. Mayra, his betrothed, even less so. Not because Mayra was the jealous type, but beautiful, unattached women couldn't dwell in men's homes they weren't acquainted with. Not unless they were a servant, and a woman of Arieen's position didn't lower herself to that humble status without serious consideration of the consequences. For if she did, she'd likely never rise above that station again.

"I could work there." Arieen grabbed his forearm, her enthusiasm growing as the idea took root. "Be a chamber or scullery maid. Or a governess? Does your cousin have children?" With an irritated huff, she pushed her hair away from her face. "I can muck stalls or dig weeds. Or do the laundry if need be."

Not with those soft, white, surprisingly strong hands. The memory of her palm pressing into his back, urging him nearer as they kissed sent a fresh jolt of heat through him. At some point, she'd removed her gloves, and her neatly-trimmed nails and unblemished fingers bespoke a life of being waited upon.

One foot on the St. Giles Cathedral's bottom riser, Coburn shook his head.

The breeze blew the cloud covering the half-moon away, and a single moonbeam slanted from the heavens, its silvery ray shining on her. Almost as if God had anointed her with His finger.

"Lass, it's nae my place to retain staff, and if 'twas, I'm guessin' ye've nae experience at menial tasks."

She turned her head, such supplication in her turned-up eyes, he guessed what she was going to ask. And damn his eyes, he knew his answer, too.

"Could you ask him, anyway, Coburn? Please?"

Chapter Ten

An hour later, ensconced in Logan's study, Coburn sipped his whisky and lounged in a worn chair before the fire. Usually when he and Logan took their respective seats in here, the conversation was amiable, even jovial.

Not tonight.

Stifling a yawn, Coburn raised his glass. Through the umber liquid, he admired the bright, frolicking flames. Exhaustion settled upon him like a warm, woolen plaid, and he struggled to keep his eyes open. Never an early riser, he'd have a devil of a time prying himself from his mattress at dawn.

Having been provided tea and a light repast by a surprisingly chipper Armstrong, the butler, Arieen awaited them in the salon. The last he'd glimpsed her through the cracked doorway, she stared at the opening, her expression hopeful and anxious.

He couldn't erase her bonnie eyes pleading with him to ask Logan to hire her. Logan hadn't funds to spare. He was barely keeping Lockelieth afloat. She'd have to work for her food and board, and he'd vow she'd never done a thing for herself her entire life.

"Ye mean to tell me, after ye congratulated me on my happy news tonight, ye compromised a lass ye just met and then proposed to her?" Logan stared at Coburn expectantly and gave an impatient jerk of his hand. "Do I have it right?"

Coburn lifted a shoulder. "More or less."

Logan tossed back his remaining whisky, then looked around rather desperately for the decanter.

As he hitched a leg over the chair's arm, Coburn pointed to the desk. "Ye left it there."

Scowling, Logan lifted the crystal topper and aimed it at Coburn. "*Ye,* who swore he'd *never* take a wife, could verra well be wed before *I* am? Since when did ye become chivalrous and noble?"

Coburn wisely stifled the chuckle rising to his throat. He'd flummoxed his cousin, and right properly. "Logan, the lass disna want to marry me."

"Smart on her part. I applaud her intelligence," Logan muttered, cross as a wounded boar.

Canting his head while he swung the leg hanging over the chair's arm, Coburn considered his cousin. What had Logan so peeved?

That he'd been roused from his bed?

That Coburn had proposed to Arieen?

"I'd no' wed ye either, ye womanizin' rake." With a harsh *clank,* Logan topped the decanter.

"Thank ye for yer confidence in me, Cousin."

Coming to stand before Coburn, his banyan rippling around his bare feet and thunder in his face, Logan merely stared, utterly baffled. His robe gaped slightly and giving an irritated huff, he jerked it closed with one hand. Evidently, he'd vaulted from his bed, naked as a selkie, when his butler had announced Coburn was at his door at twelve-thirty in the morning with a life-and-death crisis.

Life and death.

Coburn had insisted Armstrong use that precise phrase. Rotten of Coburn since he knew Logan couldn't ignore something so serious.

'Twasn't a lie exactly. More of an exaggerated truth.

Arieen's life *could* be in danger, and she *might* be facing death if she didn't find a place to live. Both were certain if she was forced to the streets.

The look on Logan's face after he'd bounded down the stairs and tore into the drawing room, skidding to a halt when he spied Arieen, resulted in a suppressed chuckle now.

Coburn had busted out laughing then, too.

"Do leave off yer juvenile snickerin'." Logan sat in the other chair, then crossed an ankle over his knee, careful to keep his nakedness concealed. "Why did ye bring her here? Ye didna need my permission to do somethin' stupid and rash. Ye've already done that."

"This from the mon who pretended to be me and lied to his betrothed about it?"

Coburn stretched his legs out, crossed his ankles, and letting his head fall back onto the chair's high back, exhaled a long breath. *God, I'm tired.* He cut Logan a sideways glance from beneath hooded eyes. "I dinna think either of us should be pointin' fingers at the other, Cousin."

Logan gave a hearty sigh.

"Aye. Ye're right." His glass resting on his thigh, Logan ran his forefinger around the rim. "What do ye need from me?"

Coburn gave in to the urge to close his heavy eyelids. "The lass wants to ken if ye'll give her a position at Lockelieth. Her father disowned her after our kiss, and she has nowhere else to go."

"Truly?" Logan's banyan swished, indicating he'd changed position. "It must've been quite a kiss."

"Aye, he truly did, and 'twas only a wee kiss." But utterly shattering in its intensity.

"Hmph. I'll bet."

"Berget Jonston offered her a place to stay tonight," Coburn said. "Against Lady Stewart's wishes, I might add. But 'twas only for one night. Lady Stewart is afraid of Arieen's father." So was most of Scotland. "I also need the carriage and funds to return to Lockelieth if ye agree to hire her."

The robust fire didn't cause the heat skating up Coburn's neck to his cheeks. Humiliating as hell to have to ask Logan for money when his pockets weren't deep either.

Coburn cracked an eye open and met his cousin's dubious green-brown eyes, so like his own. "Ye should ken her da is Robert Flemin'."

Logan's jaw unhinged, and his wide-eyed gaze flew to the partially open door. "Shite."

"Exactly."

Snapping his mouth closed, Logan veered his focus back to Coburn. "I dinna suppose she's ever worked a day in her life?"

"Nae. I dinna think so. But she says she's willin' to learn. And for food and board only." He eyed his near empty glass. Dare he indulge in another?

"Consider it done. Still, I canna help but think this disna bode well for either of ye." Logan cleared his throat, and Coburn opened his eyes a fraction again.

He recognized the expression on his younger cousin's face all too well. Logan was about to lecture him. "Ye've somethin' ye need to say?"

"I willna have ye keepin' her as yer mistress, Coburn. She'll be a servant, and ye canna take advantage of that. I dinna need the likes of her da breathin' down my neck either." He tapped his Adam's apple. "A mon like him can ruin everythin' I've been workin' for. Ye ken, men of Flemin's ilk havena a qualm about seeking vengeance."

Logan's dream was to restore Lockelieth and make her productive once more. He also intended to mine a portion of the land he gained by marrying Mayra. A few words here and there, and Fleming could throw a huge cog in those wheels.

Coburn adjusted his position on the chair so that his feet were planted on the floor. "Ye ken I've never kept a mistress, and I dinna intend to start now. Besides, Flemin' told Arieen she wasna his progeny before abandonin' her at the ball. She truly has nowhere to go."

"What a heartless bastard." Eyes narrowed the merest bit, Logan cocked his head. "Does it bother ye she willna marry ye?"

Aye, it does, but it shouldna.

Coburn took a swallow, relishing the gradual burn to his belly before answering. "No' really. As ye said, I never want to marry. If ye'll give her a place to live, I dinna have to feel guilty, nor do I have to shackle myself to a coddled chit for the rest of my life. Nae kiss is worth that sacrifice."

Hers might've been.

"The feeling is mutual, Mr. Wallace, and it's a relief to know neither of us will be saddled with that most unpleasant burden."

Coburn and Logan jerked upright as Arieen, her movements sleek and graceful, slipped into the study.

Och, hell's bloody bells. Chagrin kicked Coburn in the ribs.

From her stiff posture and starchy glances, she'd heard him.

"Please forgive the intrusion," she said, her demeanor not the least repentant. "But as 'tis already nearly one of the clock in the morning, I must have an answer. I cannot expect the Stewarts to await my arrival much longer."

They'd probably given up on her coming long ago, truth to tell.

Her troubled gaze met Coburn's.

Och, the thought had crossed her mind as well.

Compassion for her plight jockeyed for position against regret for her overhearing his callous remark. His blasted pride had been speaking, and there was no undoing the damage his words caused.

Logan placed his glass on the side table and discreetly tugged his robe over his legs, making himself more respectable.

She didn't seem to notice. Her shoulders drooped from fatigue, and Coburn swore her lashes were spikier than they'd been earlier.

Had she been crying?

Was she the type to hide her tears and only cry when alone?

Not once during this ordeal had Arieen complained, whined, or ranted about her circumstances. If she'd succumbed to tears in private, he couldn't fault her, and her fortitude earned his admiration.

"Miss Flemin', I've agreed to employ ye at my keep. I honestly dinna ken what my staff may need help with, but Mrs. Granger will assign ye yer duties. Because ye've nae experience, I'll pay ye half-wages for the first six months."

Coburn shot Logan a surprised glance. He should've known his cousin wouldn't take advantage and not pay her.

"Ye'll be provided two uniforms, and have Sunday afternoons off." Logan rubbed an eyebrow, his weariness apparent as well. "I'd offer ye a chamber above stairs, but I fear it would incite jealousy, and ye're already goin' to have to prove yerself to the rest of the help."

Hands neatly clasped before her, nothing about Arieen suggested she was anything but a cultured lady. She dipped her head, the movement at once elegant and acquiescent. "Thank you, my lord."

"Well then, I'm to bed." Logan slapped his hand on the chair's arms and pushed to his feet. He pulled the bell and a moment later Armstrong entered. Probably hovering in the corridor wishing they'd get on with it so he could seek his bed once more.

Coburn couldn't blame him. A servant's life—even with the most generous and aimable employer—wasn't easy.

"Sir?" Armstrong's ability to keep his attention riveted on Logan, despite the obvious tension in the air, was admirable.

"Please see that a bed in the servants' quarters is readied for Miss Flemin'." Logan indicated Arieen with a sweep of his hand.

One of the servant's bushy brows shied upward.

There was no help for it. Arieen couldn't sleep in the parlor, giving her a bedchamber would ignite a firestorm of rumors that neither Logan or Coburn wanted to deal with, and arriving at the Stewarts at this ungodly hour wasn't done.

Logan leveled the butler a bland don't-get-any-wrong-ideas look. "She's to be the new maid-of-all-work at Lockelieth and will depart with my cousin after breakin' her fast in the mornin'."

At least Coburn didn't have to rise before the sun. One bright spot in all of this chaos.

"Indeed, sir." His doubt as tangible as the glimmering tapers in the candelabra, the butler left.

Pale but poised, Arieen fingered her sword. She knew as well as Coburn did that by tomorrow afternoon, everyone who was anyone would have learned Arieen Fleming, disowned daughter of rich-as-Croesus Robert Fleming, had been reduced to a lowly maid-of-all-work at a crumbling Highland keep.

Her composure further earned his respect.

"I'm loath to ask, but might I impose upon you further, my lord?" Her tentative smile revealed her discomfiture.

"If I can, Miss Flemin'. What do ye require?" Logan slid Coburn a questioning glance, but he hitched a shoulder.

He hadn't a clue what she wanted either.

She traced her sword's sheath with her fingertips, revealing she wasn't as collected as she'd have them believe.

"I have need of paper and ink, so I can let Berget know why I didn't come tonight and also to tell my fa—that is, Robert Fleming, where to send my belongings. Naturally, the missives cannot be sent until morn, but I anticipate the footman delivering them might bring me word of my stepmother's labor. Or if the bairn has been born yet and how they both fare."

In the midst of her own troubles, she worried for her less-than-kind stepmother and the babe. Arieen Fleming had a pure heart. She also didn't display the temperament a spoiled lass usually did. She'd accepted her reduction in circumstances with poise and grace.

Yet, she rejected Coburn's suit without even giving him any consideration. He couldn't help but wonder if *it was* because of his lowly status despite her protests she wanted to choose her own husband. Best wait until he knew how she fared as the lowest ranking servant at Lockelieth before raining anymore accolades upon her.

"Of course. I'll have them brought to—" Logan paused. Head tilted, he considered her. "Miss Flemin', can ye calculate sums and keep records?"

Her gaze snapped to Logan's, and her long, slender fingers stilled upon her sword's sheath.

Coburn didn't like the slightly cunning expression glinting in Logan's eyes. No, he did not.

"Yes, my lord. I am well educated, and I spent three years in London learning social etiquette and decorum."

"Och, I wondered at yer perfect English," Logan said, something like gleeful satisfaction lighting his eyes.

Hope bloomed across her face. "Have you need of a governess?" The glance she sliced Coburn was just slightly short of triumphant, and pity swept him. Logan had no need for a governess. "I play two instruments and speak three languages. I have studied geography—"

Logan raised his hand, palm outward. "Nae, no' a governess, but a secretary of sorts."

CHAPTER ELEVEN

Lockelieth Keep, Scottish Highlands
One Week Later

COBURN DESCENDED THE last stair as a flash of scarlet disappeared down the corridor, revealing Arieen was already about her duties. Never had a woman distracted him as much as she did, and he found himself hard put to resist pulling her into his arms and kissing her breathless each time he encountered her.

Which, given they lived beneath the same roof, occurred multiple times daily.

His common sense scolding him soundly for yielding to temptation, he followed her to the study. She'd left the door open, and he took a few moments to savor observing her.

Lower lip caught between her teeth, and holding her spectacles in one hand, she drew the candlestick nearer as she peered at the ledger. The feminine writing desk she sat at had been his mother's. He'd asked the piece be placed before a bookshelf near the fireplace, so she wouldn't become chilled in the dark and drafty chamber.

Another, more selfish reason had motivated him to offer the desk's usage, and moving it into the study, rather than her chamber or the library. The days he worked in here, she'd be but a few feet away. He'd begun to crave her presence, much like a tippler lusted after his rum. A disturbing and growing addiction. One he wouldn't easily be able to resist.

"How is my mother's desk workin' out for ye?" he asked from the doorway.

Jumping, she dropped her spectacles and nearly toppled the inkwell, too. "You startled me, Coburn. I didn't expect you this morning. I thought you were training the horses again today."

He ambled in and after crossing to her, ran a finger over the desk's burnished wood. "I saw ye scurryin' in here and couldna resist followin' ye."

"Oh."

At his admission, her eyes went soft, and her pretty lips parted.

He stepped around the desk and resting a hip on the edge, mere inches from her, picked up her spectacles. "Have I told ye how adorable ye look wearin' these?"

Lifting them to eye height, he squinted and peered through the lenses. Everything was blurry.

"I don't think adorable is how I'd describe how I appear in them." Forming a moue with her mouth, she wrinkled her nose. "More like a frumpy spinster or a stuffy bluestocking."

She accepted them from him and, after carefully laying them atop the ledger, gazed up at him. "Did you need something?"

What would she do if he asked for a kiss?

Just a wee one?

Nae. No' wise.

Logan had warned him away from her.

"Nae. I just wanted to make sure ye're adjustin' to Lockelieth and dinna have need of anythin'." His fabricated excuse sounded feeble even to his ears.

Her bright smile lit her eyes, yet sadness also lurked in their green depths. "I'm well content."

"Have ye had any word from Flemin' about the bairn?" he asked, more as an excuse to linger than any real interest in anything related to the mean-spirited Scot.

She shook her head, and her hair—worn down today and held back with a black ribbon across her brow—billowed around her shoulders. "I know nothing other than Morag was still in labor when the footman retrieved my belongings."

"Sorry I am for ye." Coburn covered her hand with his palm. "I ken ye received a couple of letters yesterday. I'd hoped one was word about the child. I ken ye've fretted on the matter."

Arieen had a compassionate heart. And a commendable sense of duty. The staff already adored her.

"Those were from Berget and Emeline." She sat back in her chair and fiddled with the edge of her plaid shawl. Gazing up at him through her lashes, she asked, "Are you always so concerned with others' welfare?"

Flashing her what he hoped was a boyish grin, he twitched the end of her quill. "I try to be." He winked then. "But I am most especially when it comes to ye, lass."

In a subtle test, he bent his head nearer.

She didn't turn her face away, but instead dropped her focus to his lips.

Precisely the answer he sought.

Satisfaction burgeoned behind his breastbone.

He touched his mouth to hers—a tender sweep, nothing more—then framed her delicate jaw between his thumb and forefinger.

"I'd see ye happy, Arieen."

Her lashes fluttered open, and she stared into his eyes for a second.

"I have days when I am, and staying busy helps. I've learned to make cock-a-leekie soup and bread." Her cheeks turned rosy, and he withdrew his hand. "Mrs. McIntyre's been most kind and is teaching me how to cook."

"Ye want to learn how to cook?" He folded his arms, and chin lowered, regarded her.

She gave an animated nod. "Aye. And anything else the others have time to teach me."

"Ye, Arieen Flemin' are a captivatin' and confoundin' wonder." Coburn put a bent knuckle to her satiny cheek. "Are ye sure ye willna marry me? Some say I'm charmin'." He waggled his eyebrows.

"I..." She blinked and darted her gaze around the study, then straightened and donned a prim mien. "I've seen firsthand how charming you are, Coburn Wallace." She folded her arms, one ebony brow cocked wryly. "I'm willing to bet there's a long list of other lasses who've personally experienced those charms."

"I was but teasin' ye, lass."

He winked and stood, hiding how her rejection stung. He'd not make the mistake again. She might enjoy his kisses, but she wasn't ever going to consider him for a husband. She might be a servant now but, in her heart, she'd always be a lady, and ladies didn't marry the likes of him. "I'll leave ye to yer work."

Before he stepped into the corridor, realization slammed into him, stealing his breath.

He hadn't been teasing at all.

Maybe the time had come to bid Logan and Lockelieth farewell after all.

ANOTHER THREE WEEKS passed, and Arieen had settled into a comfortable routine. She hummed and tapped the toes of one foot as she studied the ledger. Even after all this time, Coburn's thoughtfulness and generosity at permitting her to use his mother's desk touched her.

She glanced to the grudging light filtering through the trio of mullioned windows along the study's south side. The torrential rain of the past two days had finally stopped, but laden clouds rendered the sky a cranky gray. Hopefully, the roads weren't impassible. Mayra Findlay and her family were due to arrive tomorrow for her wedding in a fortnight to Laird Rutherford.

Coburn and one of the clansmen walked past the windows. Head angled to hear what the Scot said, he glanced inside.

Arieen's heart hurtled to her throat. She smiled and gave a finger wave, promptly feeling daft for doing so. Until he gave her one of his wolfish grins and a wicked wink.

Of all the ridiculous things, a thrill of sensation pulsed through her.

She watched until his impressively wide back was out of sight. How often did she do that of late? Like a moon-eyed lass, she covertly stole peeks at him whenever she had the chance.

There'd been no more delicious kisses from him, more was the pity.

That day, three weeks ago when he'd asked her if she was sure she wouldn't marry him, she'd almost said maybe she would. Until she realized he jested. Her hesitation had saved her great humiliation.

Shivering, she tucked the plaid shawl snugger around her shoulders. The fireplace behind her crackled with a hearty fire, but the medieval castle's crude stones sucked the heat from the high-ceilinged room. From her very bones, too.

Bending to her task once more, she calculated the sums again and pulled a face.

Was that number a seven or a nine?

Her spectacles made the task easier, and she gave a small smile while adjusting them atop the bridge of her nose. Thank goodness they'd been among the items in the single valise filled with her possessions the footman had brought her in Edinburgh.

From the odd assortment stuffed in the satchel, a maid had hastily packed it, shoving as much in as would fit. She'd thought to include Arieen's brush, comb, and jewels. Not that she had many. Only a few pieces that had been her mother's, including a striking ruby and heart-shaped pearl brooch adorned with hugging doves.

A wonder Robert hadn't confiscated them. Perhaps he'd been too preoccupied with his wife's labor or, mayhap he hadn't seen the maid stuff the gems in Arieen's satchel.

A wistful sigh escaped her. He'd been looking for an excuse to rid himself of her, and he'd found it. It hurt though. Immeasurably. Moisture blurred her eyes, and her nostrils tingled from the tears that threatened.

Arching her back, Arieen closed her eyes and pinched the bridge of her nose above her spectacle's wire. She refused to shed more tears over the matter or wallow in self-pity. She had a position now, and must do her utmost to assure she kept it.

If she didn't...

Nae, 'tis unthinkable.

Logan Rutherford had gone well outside the bounds by retaining her for what was surely a man's position. He'd assigned her—a complete stranger—with tasks that should've been reserved for a trusted *male* secretary.

Arieen set the ledger aside while drawing another, bulkier volume before her. After opening the nut-brown leather cover, she found where she'd left off yesterday and studied the entry. She found she rather enjoyed the detailed work, and when her nose wasn't buried in a register, she insisted on helping with whatever tasks Mrs. Granger might need help completing.

Thus far, besides soup and bread, she'd learned to make oatmeal and tea, how to wash linens, polish the woodwork, and change her sheets. Her offers to help in the stables had been met with incredulous expressions and lifted brows, and thus far hadn't been accepted.

A gratified smile curved her mouth.

No one could accuse her of putting on airs. Everyone pitched in where needed at Lockelieth, including Coburn. He wore several mantles at the keep: the laird's second-in-command, steward, war chief, and several times, she'd seen him working with the horseflesh.

That was always a pleasant sight. A smile arcing her mouth, she glanced through the windows toward the stables. At that moment, a groom passed by, leading the draft horse she'd seen Coburn training.

If only Arieen might ride again. Not since London had she sat a horse, but 'twas the lengthy rides across the Highland moors she yearned for. She'd have a hard time contriving an excuse as to why her current obligations required her to make use of Laird Rutherford's stables though.

"Tea, miss?" Bearing a tray, Mrs. Granger bustled into the study, hurtling Arieen back to the present. A sunny smile lighting her jovial face, the housekeeper *tsked*. "Ye missed the midday meal again."

She'd skipped the meal on purpose, wanting to prove she was a diligent, capable worker.

The housekeeper lifted the tray an inch. "I've a Scotch pie and shortbread, too. 'Tis still warm."

Cook's pies and shortbread were the best Arieen had ever tasted. She grinned and eagerly closed the ledger before clearing a spot atop the desk. "You spoil me, Mrs. Granger, and you ought not to. I'm a servant as well."

"Ye're talkin' mince, lass. That's pure rubbish." The housekeeper clicked her tongue and placed the tray before Arieen. "We all ken ye're a fine lady."

What else did the others know about her?

Doubtless everything.

Laird Rutherford would've had to give an explanation for her presence, particularly since he was betrothed. And no one could deny it was highly unusual for a woman to be employed as a secretary. The truth must've been revealed. Or a portion of it.

Despite Arieen's determination to make the best of her situation, mortification stung and made her cheeks tingle. Nonetheless, she donned a brave smile.

"Won't you join me, Mrs. Granger?"

Mrs. Granger clicked her tongue again. "Goodness me, nae. No' with the weddin' but days away. We've rooms to prepare and food to cook. We've hired two more footmen, a groom, three maids, and a scullery maid for the foreseeable future. There's too much needs doin' for a proper joinin' celebration."

She beamed while circling the room, first putting a book aright, then fluffing a shabby pillow, and finally adjusting a slightly lopsided painting. Mrs. Granger took her duties seriously, and despite Lockelieth's age and need for refurbishment, the keep was clean and tidy.

"What can I help with? Please, you must let me." Arieen poured the brew, inhaling the fragrant steam. "As I said yesterday, I don't think the laird will mind if I put aside the ledgers for a day or two and assist you." She wasn't positive he wouldn't object, and she'd make sure to ask this afternoon, but until she'd inquired, it couldn't hurt to offer a hand.

Mrs. Granger's round face creased in thoughtful contemplation.

"Ye receive his lairdship's permission first. Afterward, I'll assign ye tasks." She ordered the laird's desk, placing his quill just so. Stopping abruptly, she glanced up, her kind face crinkled. "Oh, and Master Coburn sent word. He'd like ye to come to the stables as soon as possible."

CHAPTER TWELVE

A BITE OF Scotch pie on her fork, Arieen paused.

"Did he say why?"

Coburn had never summoned her before.

Was that why she'd seen him outside the study earlier?

The housekeeper lifted a shoulder as she toed a stray coal back toward the fire. "Nae, but he advises ye to dress warmly."

Mrs. Granger scanned the chamber one last time and, satisfied, bobbed her head, a twinkle in her eye. "When ye're done with Master Coburn, ye might want to peek into the kitchen. We're havin' rumbledethumps for dinner."

Besides clootie dumpling, rumbledethumps were Arieen's favorite food. "Oh, I shall for certain."

With another warm smile, the housekeeper went on her way.

Arieen ate half the Scotch pie, but curious to find out what Coburn wanted, left the rest and grabbed two shortbread biscuits before hurrying to her chamber. She'd return the tray to the kitchen later.

She'd expected to sleep in the servants' quarters, but Laird Rutherford had instructed that she be given the vacant governess' room. Arieen supposed her post was similar to a governess' station—not one of the serving staff, but not part of the family either. She was a person caught between two worlds and belonged to neither.

Her chest pulsed with a queer ache. Would she ever have a family of her own? Though Robert couldn't force her to marry anymore, as a misfit between social classes, her prospects remained few.

Coburn's face, complete with a roguish grin, sprang to her mind. Womanizers didn't marry penniless outcasts. Immediately, her conscience chided her. That was unfair. He'd been nothing but gallant and respectful to her since her arrival.

That wee kiss in the study couldn't be counted against him, since she'd basically invited it.

A half-smile curving her mouth at the warm memory, she opened her wardrobe. Only one outer garment had been amongst her belongings, a simple black woolen cloak. After she'd secured the clasps at her neck, she popped the last of the buttery shortbread in her mouth.

A few moments later, she exited the keep.

A bailey lay before her, and several clansmen went about their tasks. A sturdy wee pony attached to a cart waited patiently for whomever had left him there, and a few chickens clucked and pecked the ground.

She recalled from her bedchamber's view, the stables lay to the west of the inner courtyard. Having stayed inside the keep since her arrival, Arieen turned in a slow circle to get her bearings. There. The roofs of two barns obstructed the horizon.

Mindful not to step in puddles or the occasional animal droppings, she swiftly made her way across the cobblestones, all the while looking about. The people at Lockelieth were an industrious lot, and the bailey was clean and orderly, though several structures could benefit from repairs.

As she strode past, men and women nodded or offered smiles, while others bent their heads near and murmured.

A chilling thought caused a hitch in her stride. Did they know why she was here?

What did it matter? She'd bid her reputation farewell at McCullough's ball. She had a chance to prove herself here. And she would, by jimble.

Approaching the stables, she glanced around.

A pair of Scots filled a wagon with what looked to be soiled straw from the stalls, and another two chatted in the paddock, where a handful of sheep huddled in a corner. In the crisp, green meadows beyond, shaggy Highland cattle milled about in one pasture, and fluffy sheep clustered together in another. In the field nearest the keep, horses grazed, including the magnificent animal Coburn worked with.

"Afternoon, Miss Flemin'." A groom walked past, leading two saddled horses.

"Good afternoon, Lachlan."

Stepping through the open double doors, she blinked against the sudden dimness. Familiar odors: straw, horses, and liniment met her nose. Inhaling a deep breath, she savored the comforting smells.

Sharp pangs of homesickness cramped her lungs and tears smarted behind eyes. She'd put on a brave front, but the truth was, Robert's renouncement had devastated her.

After a moment, her eyes cleared of moisture and grew accustomed to the faint light.

Coburn was nowhere in sight.

"Coburn?"

"I'm in here." His coppery head appeared a few stalls down. A wide grin dividing his face and his eyes alight with excitement, he motioned to her. "Come. I want ye to see this."

Curious what could have him acting like a laddie, she drew near. Nothing was visible from her angle but, as she stepped closer, a regal sorrel whickered softly.

Coburn's hot gaze slid over Arieen, a potent caress before he dropped his attention to the floor and jutted his chin.

"Arieen, look."

An hours-old, coal-black foal with four white socks stood beside the mare.

Arieen leaned over the stall door. "Oh, Coburn. She's absolutely lovely." She shifted her focus to the mare. "And you are, too, Mum. Well done you, lass."

"That's Una." He bent and ran a suntanned hand down the foal's side. "This wee lass disna have a name yet. Logan wants Mayra to name her. She's to be the new mistress' horse. A weddin' present."

"What a wonderfully thoughtful gift." The laird truly loved his lady. The tiniest twinge of envy poked her. Not about the gift, but being adored like the laird's betrothed. Arieen promptly tamped it down, and mentally kicked a wee bit of dirt over it. Ugly thoughts and rumination led to ugly behaviors and words.

Coburn gave her a sideways look and put one long finger to his lip. "Dinna say anythin'. 'Tis a secret. Logan wasna sure the wee one would arrive in time."

"I shan't say a word. I'm sure Mayra will be thrilled."

Arieen would've been.

She retreated a step as he made to open the stall door, and her cloak snagged on a splinter midway down.

Coburn gave the partition a nudge.

"Wait, I'm caught." She only had one cloak, and she'd rather not have to mend it. Bending at the waist, she gently worked the fabric free. "There. Not even a snag."

Smiling in approval, she raised her eyes.

Like that night at the ball, their gazes tangled and held fast. Once more, she couldn't look away—didn't want to look away—from the raw hunger in his eyes.

Dark green rimmed the outside of his irises and as they gazed into each other's eyes, a connection, almost a physical bond, zipped between them. With supreme effort, she lowered her eyes, only to encounter his splendid, flawless mouth.

Lord help her, she wanted to kiss him again.

"Arieen." He breathed her name, a reverent, seductive purr, and tenderly palmed her cheek.

Laird and saints *and* angels help her.

"Do ye ken yer eyes are sparklin' with longin', *leannan*?"

He pressed his mouth to her forehead, her nose, and finally her lips.

A teasing wisp, which only made her crave more.

She clutched at the door, her legs gone soft as warm marmalade.

He'd put her right off her stride, he had. Oh, the rakish devil. Right when she thought she was on a solid path, he rocked her world, tipped her off that precarious perch she'd been balancing on for weeks.

She had feelings for this man. Strong feelings she could no longer deny.

Arieen might've said she was relieved to not be forced into marriage with him—and she was—but that didn't change the fact that he stirred something in her which had never been previously awakened.

Her femininity screeched at her to give in, to yield to the attraction.

She'd heard the laird order Coburn to leave her be, to not make her his mistress. She'd lose her position for certain if she succumbed to this madness.

The risk was simply too great.

Deliberately shutting her eyes to block the oh-so-tempting desire on his face, she took an ungraceful wobbly clomp backward and managed to swiftly spin away.

He chuckled, that irritating, delicious low rumble, and the gate clicked shut behind her. "I'll be back later, Una, to check on ye and yer bairn."

Arieen kept her back to him. Wiser that way. Less enticing.

For in moments like these, when she looked at him, and recognized the undeniable longing in his eyes, all rational thought flitted away like thistledown caught in the wind.

"Mrs. Granger said you wanted to see me, Coburn?" She wrapped her ungloved hands in the cloak's fold. Gloves hadn't been included in the valise, and the cost of new ones was too dear to contemplate right now. "Was it about the foal? If so, I thank you for thinking of me, but I should return to my duties."

The laird was due back from Glenliesh Village soon, and his new secretary shouldn't be found dallying with his cousin.

She started when Coburn took her elbow. "I thought ye might enjoy a ride. I dinna ken why I didna think of that before."

Oh, nae ye dinna.

Time alone with him was the last thing she needed at the moment. "I'm not sure the laird—"

"Logan already gave his consent, and Mrs. Granger told me ye said ye'd put aside yer work to help with the weddin' preparations. So ye canna claim ye've too much to do." Coburn continued to lead her toward the paddock.

Mrs. Granger, the sly dear. She contrived the whole thing. Was she trying to play matchmaker? Or was Coburn such a rogue the aged housekeeper couldn't resist his charms?

They emerged, and Arieen blinked from the brightness this time. More blue skies filled the heavens and pristine white clouds mixed with pewter ones.

Lachlan waited for them, holding the horses' reins.

"Badly done of you, Mr. Wallace," Arieen chided.

"Dinna get yer feathers ruffled, lass," Coburn whispered in her ear. "I was tryin' to please ye. Ye've been workin' hard since ye arrived, no' takin' yer half-days."

She stopped mid-stride and gave him an incredulous look. "Where would I have gone? I don't know anyone here."

"Aye, that's true." He guided her to the horses. "I've nae chance to be with ye alone," he murmured low.

One hand on the mount's mane, she sliced him a startled glance.

He'd wanted to be alone with her?

She shouldn't be thrilled, but she was.

More than thrilled.

Dinna be a bampot, Arieen Gillian Kinna Flemin'.

Rogues like Coburn Wallace know exactly what to say to woo lasses into their beds. Giving him a strident look, she assumed her most prim air.

"One short ride, Mr. Wallace. This isn't to become a habit."

She permitted him to hand her into the saddle. While she arranged her skirts and cloak before pulling the hood over her head, he mounted his horse.

They rode in contented silence for several minutes, and Arieen had to admit 'twas delightful. She'd always preferred the Highlands' tranquil air and slower pace.

Life was simpler here. Easier. Less complicated.

A startled red grouse took wing and as the bird flew away, Arieen took in her surroundings. Heavily-budded purple heather covered the moorlands. This might not be the home of her childhood, but anywhere in the Highlands would always feel that way. This was where she belonged, even if 'twas as a disgraced woman.

She smiled at Coburn's wide back as he rode slightly ahead of her.

"Thank you, Coburn, for insisting I join you. I appreciate this more than I can say. I've missed riding in the Highlands."

He slowed his gelding until they were side by side. Resting his forearm on his thigh, he ran his fingers along the reins as he gazed out over the landscape. Fine auburn stubble covered his angular cheeks and jaw.

"Look, Arieen," he said softly, pointing to a rocky slope.

Turning her head, she stifled a gasp. Magnificent and majestic, a white stag stood amongst the heather and boulders, his head gloriously raised and the tips of his antlers glimmering from the sunlight.

"I didn't think white harts truly existed," she whispered, unable to look away.

"There've been rumors of sightin's for years, but this is the first time I've seen him." Awe rendered Coburn's tone husky. He spoke from the side of his mouth. "Do ye ken the legend of the white stag?"

Arieen gave the slightest nod, afraid of startling the animal. "Aye. I've heard he's a symbol for the quest for spiritual knowledge."

"That, and his appearance is said to bring change to the lives of those who encounter him. I've never been much into superstitions, but today..." He paused, and an inflection in his voice caused her to give him an acute look.

The stag bolted at her sudden movement, and a distressed sound escaped her. "Och, nae. I could've watched him for hours."

"Me as well." With a click of his tongue, Coburn urged his horse forward.

Wouldn't it be something if the stag's sighting truly was providential?

They rode in silence for several more minutes. Occasionally, a bird flew off or a hare bolted across the path.

"Coburn? Does it ever bother you Laird Rutherford owns all of this?" She made a sweeping gesture. "And you work for him?"

"Nae. He was born to it, and I wasna. I'm happy doin' what I do. Besides, he's like a brother to me, and he treats me as an equal." He shook his head. "Nae, I dinna begrudge him, and I'm thankful to no' have the responsibility he carries."

He straightened in the saddle and surveyed the cottages dotting the landscape.

"All of these people rely upon him. On his protection and leadership." He swept a hand before him. "'Tis nae easy burden to bear. I do what I can to ease it, but I dinna want to take his place."

"That says a lot about you, and I think he's fortunate you live at the keep, too." She swatted at an insect buzzing around her face. "I haven't any cousins."

"Or kin either?"

Though his question was casual, she angled her head and gave him a searching look. "Not that I'm aware of."

Scraping a hand through his hair, he breathed out a long breath. "We have a problem, lass." He veered her a short, serious glance. "Which is the other reason I wanted to get ye away from the keep."

Queer disappointment wrestled with accusation. She should've known he was up to something. Almost a month, and he just now decided to take her riding? More fool she.

She studied his taut jaw, tense shoulders, and the four lines wrinkling his forehead. An undeniable nuance of tension hovered about him. The thought plucked at her already-frayed nerves.

This was the same solemn man who'd tried hard to persuade her to marry him.

The same man who said he was glad no' to have to shackle himself to a coddled chit.

Arieen also slowed her horse, apprehension unmercifully digging its nasty pointed claws into her spine. Had the laird told Coburn to dismiss her? Already?

Anxiety knotted her belly.

What had she done?

Wracking her brain, she tried to recall a misstep or breach of decorum she'd committed.

"A problem?" Squeezing the reins, she pulled her brows together. "Have I done something wrong? Committed an offense?"

Or maybe the laird worried about his new bride associating with a tarnished woman. Wouldn't he have considered that before retaining Arieen? Did he regret the impulse now? Or… possibly Miss Findlay didn't want another woman working closely with her husband. Arieen couldn't fault her on the latter, which was why females were rarely employed in such positions.

"Nae, ye havena done anythin'." Coburn blew out another breath, and cupped his nape, his expression compassionate. Or did contriteness darken his eyes to the color of mulled cider?

"What does that mean? Either I have or I haven't."

"I warned Logan before we left Edinburgh," he said, staring off into the horizon.

"Warned him about what?" she managed to ask between numb lips, terrified of his answer. Her heart beating a staccato rhythm against her rib cage, she clenched her reins between shaky fingers. After all, what could be so awful he looked like he'd swallowed hot coals?

"He didna think 'twas an issue." Was it her overwrought nerves, or did his demeanor appeared almost apologetic? "Because he's to be wed soon. But with Mayra arrivin' tomorrow and the whispers increasin', ye need to ken."

For God's sake.

Would the infuriatin' mon spit out whatever he had to say?

"Please speak plainly. What whispers?" She tilted her head and pursed her lips. "Coburn, are there suggestions there is something untoward going on between the laird and me?"

If so, everything was ruined.

Was the gossip so very unexpected?

Nae.

Naturally she couldn't continue on if such was the case. It made sense though, and that was why she'd never understood why he'd offered her the position in the first place. But to have this hope, this reprieve, snatched from her...

Brows high on his forehead, Coburn pinched the bridge of his nose, so obviously discomfited, if this situation wasn't so bloody awful, she might've giggled.

"Mary, Joseph, and Jesus, Coburn. What. Is. It?"

"Lass..." Taking her hand, he cupped it in his callused palm, running his thumb over her knuckles.

Trailing the soothing movement with her gaze, she fought for composure. "Can I presume a certain pompous viscount has made a point to defame me all over Edinburgh? And that it's taken a remarkably short amount of time for the chatter to reach the Highlands?"

She meshed her lips against the foul oath thrumming there.

"Aye, almost as if someone deliberately spread the gossip and embellished the sordid details, draggin' Logan into the muck, too." Coburn gave her fingers a gentle squeeze. "A few nasty-minded folks have suggested ye are Logan's mistress, and to protect him and Mayra, I said..."

Leveling him a wooden stare, she yanked her hand away.

She could barely form the words through her stiff lips.

"You told them I was *your* mistress?"

CHAPTER THIRTEEN

COBURN JERKED HIS head up.

"Nae, I'm no' that much of an arse." He made a brusque motion toward his chest. "I told them I proposed to ye in Edinburgh. I also said ye insisted on helpin' at Lockelieth, and that's why ye're assistin' Logan."

Frustration clogged Coburn's throat. He despised twisting the truth or lying, and self-loathing thrummed through his blood, both for his deception and for involving Arieen in it.

"So, I cannot accept wages, else it will look all the more suspicious." Accusation laced her voice and filled her eyes. She shook her head, and the hood slipped off. "You've left me with no recourse. None at all."

Each syllable was another sharp jab to his already guilty conscience.

He'd anticipated Arieen's anger.

After all, he'd basically entrapped her.

But devil take it, Logan loved Mayra, and she adored him. His cousin had almost lost her once, and Coburn wasn't going to stand by and let gossip, no matter how farfetched and contrived, destroy what they had.

Most people didn't care about the truth. A hint of scandal, a whispered lie, and Society tried and convicted the parties involved. He didn't give a ragman's scorn what the tongue-waggers said about him.

But their rumormongering destroying others?

That he bloody well did care about.

More fool he, but he hadn't expected Arieen's icy castigation.

She gave him a wintery glare, frigid enough to freeze his ballocks on the spot. He actually felt them shrivel inside his trews. They might've squeaked in fear, too.

Damn, but she was magnificent.

Without another word, she turned her mare around and bolted away like a banshee out of hell, her black cloak billowing behind her.

Despite the troublesome circumstances, he couldn't help but admire her fine seat and her expert horsemanship. She was a woman designed to ride.

Regret a heavy yoke upon his shoulder, he scrutinized the path she had disappeared down. Best to allow her to calm a bit before pursuing the matter—for he must. The truth of it was, he told the gabble jaws his wedding was next week. The longer an unwed woman of her station remained beneath Lockelieth's roof, the more difficult it would be to undo the damage.

After dismounting and leaving Ibor's reins dangling, Coburn sat on a boulder amongst the purple-tinged heather. Snapping off a blossom-laden twig from a nearby plant, he crossed his ankles.

He'd come full circle.

First, he'd proposed to Arieen to save her reputation, and for the same reason and to protect Logan, Coburn had announced she was his betrothed.

The matter might seem trivial, but it wasn't.

While a man keeping a mistress was commonplace, a laird moving his paramour into his keep a fortnight before his wedding could expect sharp criticism. The clan must respect Logan. The old laird had neglected his tribe, demanded much from them, and gave nothing in return.

Dangerous discontent had burbled beneath the surface those years

Logan had been away, and a few disgruntled men yet complained amid those clansmen loyal to Logan. Both contributed to Coburn remaining at Lockelieth rather than following his dream of traveling.

He tossed the heather aside and raised his face to the sky, soaking in the warm rays intrepidly shining between the clouds.

Since when had he become such a bloody saint?

The truth of it was, he wouldn't mind taking Arieen to wife.

Nae mind at all.

These past weeks, he'd come to enjoy her presence, her ready wit, and keen intelligence. He'd also taken a goodly number of frigid dips in the burn beyond the stables. She'd set his blood afire with their kiss at the ball, and his passion had simmered hot and fierce since.

But how to convince her he *wanted* to wed her?

In a week, to boot?

Coburn couldn't profess undying love.

She was too astute to fall for false sentimental gibberish. Besides, he wouldn't lie to her. He'd spun numerous falsehoods of late and despised himself for it. Until now, he might've had a reputation as a rapscallion, but he was famed for his honesty.

True, he felt more affection for Arieen than he had prior females, but he wasn't a besotted fool like Logan. He was capable of concentrating and carrying on a conversation without distraction—unlike his cousin of late.

Didn't that prove he wasn't enamored?

He couldn't help but grin at the memory of Logan clanging around in too-big armor at the ball, his pride kicked to the gutters in his determination to convince Mayra to have him. Logan—

Coburn's reserved, practical cousin—would've done anything, sacrificed everything for Mayra.

Coburn's humor faded.

Logan's taunt at the ball pealed in Coburn's head. "Just ye wait, Coburn. Yer day may come yet. And if it does, I'll be right there mockin' ye, rubbin' yer nose in yer warmer affections."

No, Coburn couldn't say he was madly in love with Arieen. But if he must marry, she was his choice. Besides, she had nowhere else to go, and he wouldn't allow her to be cast out again.

Could she be happy with him?

He'd do his best to ensure she was. Bedsport wouldn't be an issue. Of that, he was certain.

Passion simmered beneath her surface, and he was experienced enough to know how to release her desire. But he yearned for more than physical attraction from Arieen. Until now, he hadn't thought he desired any such thing from a woman, and he held her responsible for changing him.

He puckered his lips and, puffing out a breath, eyed his gelding.

"Och, Ibor, how do ye advise I win an unwillin' lass' heart? I've nae heavy purse to shower her with valuable baubles, nor am I a poet or an artist." He brushed a bit of heather from his thigh. "I dinna think Arieen would care for either, actually."

The horse, nibbling a bit of succulent grass, snorted and raised his head, almost as if he indicated the swath of bluebells farther along the slope.

Flowers?

Coburn shrugged. It couldn't hurt.

An hour later, he knocked at her arched chamber door, a handful of bluebells clutched in his fist.

Ibor had better be right.

She didn't answer, and he tested the handle. Unlocked. He opened the door and peeked inside.

Arieen wasn't in here.

He hadn't been in this room since he and Logan played hide-and-seek as children.

The bedchamber was tidy, but stark. Except for a hair brush and comb, along with what looked to be a small jewelry box on the dressing table, it held no signs of her personal touch or belongings.

How could it?

She'd come to Lockelieth with but a single satchel. She'd worn the same two gowns, alternating them each day, for the past weeks. Not once had he heard a complaint from her bonnie lips about her lack of gowns, bonnets, or fallals.

He laid the bluebells on her pillow.

Maybe he should've written a note, too.

A simple, sincere apology.

Did she have paper and ink in here? He twisted around to search her chamber, and pulled up short.

Wearing her cloak, Arieen stood a few inches inside the doorway. Several strands of ebony windblown hair had escaped their pins and tumbled around her face and shoulders. Desolate eyes, framed by lush, pointy sable lashes accused him.

Had she hidden away to cry again?

I've done this to her. His heart skipped a beat. *Wounded this intrepid woman.*

"What are you doing?" She looked from him to the flowers, their blue a brilliant contrast to the faded yellow coverlet atop the bed.

"Tryin' to make amends."

"A bunch of flowers cannot compensate for you lying, Coburn."

She straightened her shoulders and lifted her chin. A flicker of pain flashed in her eyes, and he wished he had another choice—one that would give her the life she deserved.

He pressed his lips together and rubbed the side of his head. "I ken, *leannan*, and I am woefully regretful."

Leaving the door open, she unfastened the clasps at her throat and wandered toward the wardrobe in the corner.

For a woman her height, she moved with a sensual, elegant grace. It struck him how much he enjoyed observing her—the slope of her swanlike neck, the elegant way she moved her hands. How she captured her lower lip when vexed or troubled, the delicate upward sweep of pink on her cheeks, and the way her right brow arched high in skepticism or humor.

After sliding the cloak from her shoulders and placing it with the other sparse contents inside the armoire, she shut the narrow door. Hands behind her back, she leaned against the wardrobe. Expressionless, she stared at him, her eyes squinted the merest bit as her gaze roved his face.

"What do ye seek, lass?"

An apology? He'd already offered a genuine one.

A different solution? Coburn couldn't contrive one.

Or did she try to discern what kind of man he was?

Right now, he wasn't certain.

The man he'd formerly been had undergone a dramatic change since meeting her, and he scarcely recognized himself in many respects.

Shoving away from the wardrobe, she dropped her attention to the stone floor.

"Arieen…"

She lifted forlorn eyes, and the hurt and betrayal there twisted his gut like a rusty blade, eviscerating him. A gasp nearly wrested from his throat at her palpable pain.

"Arieen, I…"

He tried again, but she lifted a slender hand.

"I've had time to think, and I know you were protecting the laird and Miss Findlay," she said. "Your loyalty lies with them, and I suppose you thought you were being noble—offering us like a sacrifice to ensure their happiness. I understand, although I shan't pretend to like it."

Except for her pulse ticking rapidly at the juncture of her throat, she gave no indication of her upset. Must she be calm and logical?

He'd feel better if she railed at him. Cursed or skelped him in the face. If the icy fury he'd seen earlier flamed again in her eyes, and not this defeat that had stolen the light from her face. His heart buffeted the walls of his chest, and he longed to be able to tell her not to worry. That everything would work out in the end.

But he couldn't, because it wouldn't.

Not the way she wanted things to.

"But..." She swallowed, her composure slipping. "What am I to do now?"

Ach, leannan. Ye're tearin' my heart from my chest.

Arieen rallied her comportment and continued with a degree more self-possession.

"I cannot be responsible for a wedge between the laird and his lady. He's done much for me, and I was a stranger to him. Neither shall I have you entering a marriage I know you don't desire." She stood there, wounded and fragile, her voice the merest shred of brittle sound. "Therefore, I have no alternative but to leave Lockelieth."

She'd been brave and courageous, showing such fortitude these past days. Always smiling and lending a hand wherever she could. Determined not to offend or be a burden. Yet beneath her outward bravado, she was afraid, as any woman in her position would be.

In a few long strides, his *cuaran* boot heels rapping loudly on the worn stones, he crossed to her. He gently drew her into his arms, desperate to offer her comfort.

"Nae. Ye'll no' leave. Ye'll stay and marry me, because I want to take ye to wife, and for no other reason."

"You don't want to marry me. I heard you say so." His chest grew suspiciously damp.

"I was speakin' mince out of frustration." He kissed the crown of her head. "And, I do want to wed ye, lass. Ye and no other. Ever."

Even as he spoke the words, their truth resonated within his spirit. No power on this earth could've forced him to wed Arieen unless he'd already been amenable to the idea.

"Ye can continue as Logan's secretary, if ye wish to. He'll pay ye, and ye can save the money." She didn't respond, and he made the promise he'd hoped he wouldn't have to make. "After a time, when the bletherin' has stopped and the gossips have moved on to more fertile fields, ye can file for an annulment."

With everything in his power, he'd strive to change her mind in the meanwhile.

Coburn pressed his cheek to her glossy head and breathed in her essence. Her hair was cold, and as the thought crossed his mind, she shuddered.

Offering his body's warmth, he drew her minutely nearer. Hope soared anew when she didn't promptly pull from his embrace. Today, she didn't smell of perfume, but her own clean, womanly scent. From the corner of his eye, he scrutinized the dressing table again.

No fragrance bottle?

Fleming had denied her that, too?

Horse's arse.

Och, Coburn knew what his next gift would be. He had a bit of money stashed away. Tomorrow, he'd ride to Edinburgh. In fact, he'd call upon Robert Fleming and attempt to collect the rest of her possessions.

What harm could there be in asking the dobber?

Voice thick and husky, she spoke brokenly into his chest, as if she struggled not to weep again. "Aren't annulments…practically as impossible to acquire…as a divorce?"

"Aye. I shall no' lie to ye, lass." He ran his hands along her slender spine, as much to soothe her as in guilty pleasure of touching her. "They are."

Usually a dissolution was only granted if one spouse was already married or the parties were too closely related. Or if it could be proven the marriage was never consummated. And annulments took years.

Renewed determination pelted through him. That gave him time to convince her to stay married, to show her they could be a suitable match. If he had his way, he'd never let her go—she'd want to stay with him. Forever.

She slanted her head upward, moisture making her eyes shimmering green pools in the late afternoon light. "Chances are then, ours will be a marriage until death."

Would that be awful?

He again wanted to ask, but dreaded her answer. Grazing his knuckles across one satiny cheek, he dipped his head. "Aye. I wouldna mind."

She gave a pathetic laugh, shaking her head. More tendrils slipped loose of their pins with the movement. "I've gone from being promised to a *Sassenach* whoremonger to being betrothed to a Scottish rogue."

It rankled to be compared to Quartermain, but Coburn held his tongue. He deserved her scorn. Perchance someday, he'd earn her love.

She extracted herself from his hold.

"Och, at least I'll live in Scotland and not England. There's that to be grateful for." Rubbing her arms, she peeked at him from beneath her lashes. "I don't think you'll lock me in my chamber, as Quartermain threatened to do."

The scunner probably would've beaten her.

"I do regret it's come to this, Arieen."

Her rueful, closed-mouth smile held no self-pity or enmity. "I know. And I also know I couldn't have remained in my position as the laird's secretary indefinitely." She lifted a slender shoulder. "'Tis the way of things. Women have little say about their own lives." Giving a slight shake of her head, she breathed out a resigned sigh. "Maybe someday, that will change."

"I vow, I'll be faithful to ye, lass." Coburn took her hand and raised it to his lips.

Ink stained her fingertips, and one finger had a scratch that hadn't been there yesterday.

She quirked an austere brow in amused reproof. "I'm supposed to believe a Highland rogue is redeemable?"

"I havena touched another woman since I kissed ye on the terrace."

"Almost a month?" Head canted, her arms folded across her chest, she elevated a finger toward him. "My, your restraint is admirable. Have you ever abstained that long before?"

Aye, but he wasn't discussing his previous associations with her.

A spark of mischief glinted in her eyes. That was another thing he adored about her. Her sense of humor and that she didn't sulk or pout.

"I find when it comes to ye, Arieen Flemin', I am capable of a great many things that astound me."

And confused the hell out of him as well.

Something shone in her eyes before she averted her gaze.

"I might say the same of you, Coburn."

Now wasn't the time to explore exactly what she meant. But later, he'd coax the truth from her. He suspected at least a portion of her reluctance was born from resentment that her future was being decided for her again.

Giving her an encouraging smile, he crooked a finger and placed it beneath her chin. "I shall try my best to make ye happy, lass."

"I believe you." Her gaze trailed over his face, an unwilling caress, he'd vow.

Her words gave him confidence.

Theirs might not be a love match, but they could, in time and with effort, be content. He was convinced of it.

"Ye havena given me an answer, Arieen. Will ye marry me and let me try to make amends?"

She gazed out the windows, her expression vulnerable and a trifle lost. As she was wont to do when thoughtful or anxious, she trapped the corner of her lower lip between her teeth.

He ached to taste her mouth again, to show her how wondrous passion could be, but she needed time to accept this new blow.

She swallowed perceptibly before meeting his gaze square on. "Aye, Coburn. I'll marry you."

Unforeseen happiness blared victorious celebration in his blood, but he restrained the urge to sweep her into his arms once more. This wasn't a joyful occasion for her.

"I saw Logan's horse in the stables earlier," he said. "Shall we go below and tell him our decision?"

He wasn't sure Logan would welcome the announcement, even if he could be made to understand it was for the best.

Arieen touched her hair. "As soon as I've made myself presentable."

"Of course." Coburn crossed his arms and leaned a shoulder against one of the bed's four posts.

Standing before the oval looking glass attached to the dressing table, she made quick work of repinning the errant strands.

He felt positively domesticated while watching her perform the simple act. Something a wife might do in front of her husband. What other things might a lass do before her spouse?

Undress? Bathe?

His blood quickened at the thought.

Aye, he'd have no trouble with the more intimate areas of wedlock.

"I would have your word on one thing first, Coburn." She met his gaze in the reflection.

He canted his head. "What might that be?"

"Ours is a marriage in name only." She shoved a pin into the knot at the back of her head. "We'll have a marriage of convenience. Nothing more."

Och, I dinna think so.

Unfolding his arms, he chuckled and advanced toward her. "*Lean-*

nan, I dinna think ye ken what ye're askin' me. I've wanted ye with a raw, burnin' hunger since I saw ye enter the ballroom. Ye've captured me in yer web, and I canna see anyway of escapin'."

"Coburn..." She raised a palm as if to ward him off.

He locked his gaze onto her wide, wary eyes, wrapped his arms around her waist, pulling her against his chest, and nuzzled her neck. "Ye feel somethin' for me, too. I ken it."

Her sharp intake of breath as her lashes fluttered closed told him everything he needed to know.

"Nay, I canna agree to yer request," he said. "But I vow, I'll wait until ye come to me."

Slowly, the thick fringe of her lashes lifted. "*Och*, ye braw, conceited mon. Ye'll be waitin' a verra, *verra* long time."

Bursting into laughter, he squeezed her waist. "We'll see, my bonnie lass. Let's tell Logan and decide what day next week we're to wed."

Jaw slack, she spun around, and spluttered, "Next week?"

Chapter Fourteen

FOR THE UMPTEENTH time since Coburn had departed three mornings ago, Arieen glanced to the study's windows.

Would he return today? She'd expected him yesterday. They were supposed to wed in four days.

It mystified her how much she missed him, hearing his bark of laughter and his rumbling brogue, or smiling at him in passing. She missed their conversations over dinner, and his rakish winks and cocky waves. In fact, if anyone had told her she'd ache from the longing to see him once more, she'd have said they were numpty.

But she did.

Aye, I do.

She blinked away the tears blurring her view of the ledger.

Over and over, she'd contemplated alternatives to marrying him, and no matter how creative she believed she was, it all came down to feasibility. Nothing else was. Wedding Coburn was the logical choice, all the way around.

As she'd ruminated, a more poignant truth, one she couldn't argue against, became clear.

She didn't oppose the union—not anymore. The opposite was true. She couldn't imagine a life with anyone else. But being compelled to do so, having the choice taken from her—by Odin, she found that irksome.

At night, her mind replayed his promise to make her happy. His vow to be faithful. His profession that he wanted to marry her and no other.

He'd ignited a miniscule spark of hope that he meant it.

A wry smile skewing her mouth, she shook her head at her musing. Confound the dashing Scottish swashbuckler. What had he done to her?

A soft knock preceded Miss Findlay sticking her blonde head into the study. She fairly floated into the room, her happiness evident in her radiant smile and glowing face. "I thought I'd find ye here, Arieen. Logan says ye work too hard."

Mayra and Logan's love was a wondrous thing to behold. It lifted Arieen from her doldrums.

"I hoped ye might have time this afternoon to help me decide the menu for the wedding feast." Mayra poked around Logan's desk, as a woman curious about her intended was inclined to do.

"Of course. I'd be happy to help," Arieen said, removing her spectacles.

"My brothers are off exploring." Mayra glanced upward, grinning. "Probably getting into mischief. And Mum and our lady's maid are having a lie-down."

"I've finished today's entries, so I'm free to help in any way I can." Arieen stood and arms extended overhead, she stretched, stifling a yawn.

Coburn better return soon so she could sleep at night, or she'd be stumbling around in a drowsy fog.

Mayra eyed the ornate ceiling. "Lockelieth has a rustic charm, disna it?"

"Indeed. I've marveled at the detailed workmanship many times." The keep possessed dozens of rooms and corridors Arieen longed to explore, but hadn't the audacity to do so without permission.

Mayra looped her arm through Arieen's elbow as they exited the study. "I canna tell ye how happy I am another young woman will live here. I dinna have a sister, and since Logan and Coburn are like brothers, I hope we'll be like sisters, too."

Moisture pooled in Arieen's eyes. She'd fretted Mayra wouldn't like her or would resent her presence. "I'd like that very much. I haven't any brothers or sisters."

At least none that she knew of.

Each day, Arieen continued to hope there'd be a post from Morag or Robert about their bairn. She desperately wanted to know how the child was.

"I've asked Mrs. Granger to have Cook put on the kettle and bring us tea in the maroon salon." Mayra dimpled, her light blue eyes sparkling. "I've found weddin' plannin' gives me a robust appetite. I might've requested seed cake, Scotch eggs, and shortbread, too."

Mayra's humor was contagious, and Arieen giggled. "I've never tasted better shortbread, have you?"

"Nae, and yesterday when I asked for the recipe, Mrs. McIntyre just smiled and winked." The slightest pout turned Mayra's mouth down. "She wouldna give it to me when I suggested I should probably have it as the new mistress."

"You didn't." Arieen giggled, a hand over her mouth. "That was badly done of you."

Mayra chuckled as they turned a corner down another passageway. "It was worth a try. I'll have to keep Mrs. McIntyre content if I ever hope to acquire her recipe."

Once they'd settled in the salon, Arieen studied the room. From its heavy claret-colored draperies—years out of date—to its matching shabby chairs and sofas, the chamber had once been a grand place meant to impress guests.

Though spotlessly clean, time and neglect had taken a toll. A dark, ornate mantel encased an impressive fireplace where a toasty fire crackled. A single threadbare rug covered the floor between the sofas, atop which sat a baroque walnut tea table.

She hadn't spent much time in here. Her position didn't warrant it, and Logan hadn't entertained since she'd arrived.

Arieen curved her mouth in welcome as Brewster entered with their tea.

Oh, black bun, too. Normally, the fruit cake wrapped in pastry was only served for special occasions. Mrs. McIntyre's way of making recompense for denying Mayra her famed shortbread recipe?

After placing the tray on the table, the butler faced Mayra. "Will there be anythin' else, Miss Findlay?"

"Nae, thank ye." She lifted the teapot, about to pour Arieen's cup when she paused. "Oh, wait, Brewster. Please express my gratitude to Mrs. McIntyre for the lovely tea settin'."

He dipped his head. "Verra good."

She waited until he'd gone before whispering, "Do ye think that was a wee bit too much?"

"I don't, honestly. I believe servants are taken for granted far too often." Arieen selected a sliver of black bun. "Do you expect many guests for the wedding, Mayra?"

"Nae. Logan and I want to keep the affair intimate. Lockelieth isna in a state to receive a large number of guests either." Mayra leaned back and fiddled with a pillow. "Did ye ken we were betrothed as children? He was six years old, and I was an infant."

Arieen stopped stirring her tea. "Truly? I had no idea. Was that difficult for you or did you always love him?"

"Och, nae I didna love him." Mayra's mouth tipped into a private smile. "I tried for years to get out of the contract. I only saw him once as a child and the next time we met, he pretended to be Coburn."

"He didn't!" Arieen found herself leaning forward, hanging on every word.

"He did, indeed. Although I believed he was someone else, I kent there was somethin' special about Logan. He was constantly in my thoughts. When I wasna with him, I missed him so fiercely, it hurt.

And when I saw him, my pulse did all sorts of daffy things, and my stomach felt peely-wally."

Pressing a hand to her own unsettled tummy Arieen repeated in her mind what Mayra said.

That is love?

Expression dreamy, Mayra stared into space. "I may have fallen in love with him when I tumbled off the dog cart, and he caught me. I kent for certain I loved him within a fortnight."

Jaw slack, Arieen gawked.

Mayra had described her symptoms. Right down to the waffy tummy business. Was it possible? Could she be in love with Coburn? Had it all begun with their magical kiss at the ball?

A thrill tunneled through her.

"Ye and Coburn fell in love quickly, too, didna ye?" Mayra asked.

How was Arieen supposed to answer?

Until this moment, she believed she was marrying Coburn purely to protect Logan and Mayra. She'd stumbled upon a precious secret and wanted to savor the epiphany, to cherish the novelty before she discussed it with anyone.

Straightening, Mayra gathered her writing utensils. She didn't seem to notice Arieen hadn't responded. "I feel sorry for people who never experience what we have."

"Aye. 'Tis very special," Arieen agreed.

Mayra bit into a biscuit as she arranged her foolscap and quill. She dipped the quill and, a single groove wrinkling her forehead, glanced up.

"Now, what do ye want for yer first course, Arieen?"

Arieen gathered her scattered wits. "But...I thought this was for *your* wedding. Coburn and I planned on a small ceremony with no folderol afterward."

Actually, they hadn't discussed the after part, merely the quiet joining before a cleric with Logan and Mayra as witnesses.

"Why ever would ye think that? Ye and Coburn are marryin' first."

Mayra appeared quite taken aback, and Arieen rushed to apologize.

"Forgive me, Mayra. I assumed we were discussing *your* feast. Coburn and I have no plans for a celebration."

"Of course ye must celebrate. Actually, what we should do—what would be brilliant—is to have a double weddin'." A spark ignited in Mayra's eyes, and she clapped her hands. "Aye, Arieen, we really should. How perfect would that be? It'd be much less work for the staff, too. I canna think of anythin' I'd like more. Please say ye will."

Lowering her gaze to hide the rush of grateful tears, Arieen struggled to control her emotions. Mayra's generosity overwhelmed her. "You would share your special day? We're practically strangers."

Besides, theirs would be a real, loving marriage. *I wish I were marrying for love, too.* The thought hammered her heart, and she raised her hand to her chest.

Mayra took Arieen's hand between hers. "Aye, but I kent from the first moment we were destined to be friends. How could we no'? We both love those rapscallions."

Fingering her gown, Arieen knitted her brows at the new stain above her left knee. "I haven't anything special to wear."

Mayra made a shooing motion with her hand as she eyed Arieen.

"We're about the same height and build. I'm sure I have somethin' that would fit ye. Besides, our braw men, willna care what we're wearin'." She wiggled her eyebrows naughtily. "They'll only be thinkin' of takin' off our gowns."

Mayra gave a sage nod and took another bite.

Arieen couldn't help it, she laughed. Mayra was a delight. No wonder Logan adored her.

Strident voices in the corridor drew Arieen's attention.

Was that Coburn?

He was back? Her newfound love made her belly quiver in blissful anticipation.

Until he strode in, the edges of his face all harsh planes and angles.

The anticipation frolicking in her middle turned to apprehension.

"Coburn?"

What on earth had put the thunder in his face and starch in his posture? He'd only just arrived home.

On his heels, Robert Fleming toddled in, answering her question.

Oh, God.

She slowly put her teacup down. Breath trapped in her lungs and swathed in dread and a cold sweat, she rose. Heart beating a jagged rhythm, she clasped her hands before her, squeezing her fingers to stop their shaking.

Had the bairn died, and he was here to exact more revenge?

She sent Coburn a silent entreaty for help.

"Dinna fash yerself, lass." His calm assurance washed over her. "Trust me."

She did. Always had.

Logan plowed into the parlor, his countenance only slightly less stormy than Coburn's. Clearly disgruntled, he sliced Robert a steely look. "Mayra, Mr. Flemin' requires a word with Arieen."

Arieen didn't miss the fact he hadn't asked Coburn to leave.

Curious.

Logan extended his arm, but Arieen shook her head and reached for Mayra's hand. "No, please. I'd like her to stay, my lord. You and Coburn as well."

She'd rather they were here for whatever bad news Robert was about to announce. She needed their support now more than ever.

Coburn's features softened and the force of his half-smile touched her from across the room, sending a tingle of sensation skittering down her spine.

An astute woman, Mayra stepped near and wrapped an arm around Arieen's waist.

Logan and Coburn traded an approving glance.

"I'd prefer a private audience, Arieen." Robert shuffled his feet and tugged at his collar.

Shoulders squared, she angled her chin. "And I'd prefer my friends are present. Those who took me in when you cast me out."

She drew a bracing breath and squared her shoulders, ready for any news he might bring.

Robert offered a nervous tick of a smile, his attention flitting from person to person before resting on her once more. He clawed at his neck again.

She'd never seen him this discomposed, except for the night Morag went into premature labor.

"'Tis glad I am to see ye in bonnie health, lass."

Lass?

Brow knitted, she pulled her mouth into a thin line. What went on here?

He behavior was almost…contrite.

Or wily.

She relaxed the tiniest bit, but ire promptly took anxiety's place. "My health is due to Laird Rutherford's benevolence. If it hadn't been for him, I don't know what would have become of me, since you made no effort to contact me for a month."

That wasn't true.

She and Coburn would've wed already, but out of necessity, not by choice.

As awful as the past weeks had been, she was in a position to marry him for love. If he felt the same toward her, the hardship would have been worth it. From the warm regard glowing in his eyes, he might very well have tender feelings for her.

"I kent ye were here and well cared for." Robert's voice took on the slightest belligerent tone.

"And that made it all right?" She took a calming breath. What was done was done. "Why are you here? What do you want?"

If the bairn had died, he'd have told her by now.

Robert puffed out his chest, looking every bit the proud da. "I have twin sons. Braw, healthy laddies. Samuel and Seamus."

He grasped his lapels and rocked back on his heels.

Twins. That explained Morag's enormous belly.

"Congratulations. I'm truly happy for you and Morag." And she was. Enormously relieved as well. "Perhaps someday, you'll bring them for a visit."

Not likely, but she wouldn't be churlish.

Robert scratched his temple, his former discomfit evident again. "The midwife and the doctor vowed that was why Morag went into early labor."

Much of the tension knotting Arieen's shoulder muscles eased, and she pressed a hand to her belly, almost giddy with relief.

Robert's attention swept to Logan first, then gravitated to Mayra.

He wouldn't meet Coburn's eyes.

Why?

Had Coburn coerced him into venturing to Lockelieth? Or had Coburn tried to prevent his coming?

"No' the other reason I accused ye of. I wanted ye to ken I dinna blame ye, and I regret my treatment of ye." His demeanor repentant, head bowed and hands clasped before him, Robert said, "Ye dinna deserve that, and I ask ye to forgive me."

"In time, I'm sure I shall, but right now, I'm too hurt." The wound of his harsh rejection was fresh around the edges yet.

Mayra gave Arieen's waist a little squeeze.

Lips pressed into a thin line, he dropped his gaze. "Aye, I understand."

Who was this humbled man? Arieen canted her head, doubt whispering in her ears. If she knew one thing about Robert Fleming, it was that he didn't grovel.

Not unless he had a purpose.

She narrowed her eyes. "You could've said all of this in a letter. Why travel to the Highlands when you have two newborn bairns?"

"Och, we've moved the household to the Highlands, too. Morag wanted the lads out of the city's putrid air. The wee ones are thrivin'." His obvious delight softened her heart a shred.

"I'm glad they're doing well."

Get to the point.

"That's why I was delayed returnin'." Coburn gave Robert a hard look. "When I arrived in Edinburgh and found the house closed up, I had to find out where they'd gone. I think ye'll be happy to ken we've brought the rest of yer possessions."

"Thank you." She brushed a crumb off her skirt. "I've grown weary wearing the same things."

"Aye, aye," Robert said. "The trunks have already been taken to yer chamber."

There must be something else Robert wanted. Something important, besides her forgiveness.

But what?

Arms folded, Arieen tapped her toe, impatient for whatever this was to be done. "What is the real reason you are here, Robert?"

He raised his gaze and licked his lower lip. He attempted a smile, but it looked more like a grimace or his stomach pained him.

"I've had another offer for yer hand, Arieen. A brilliant match," he said in a rush. "A Scottish duke. He saw ye at the ball and was verra taken with ye."

At last, his real reason for coming.

This visit was about Robert acquiring the title he'd coveted for so long. The knowledge plummeted her stomach to her toes. The manipulating toad. And who was this duke? The dark-haired man who'd gawked at the ball?

Robert warmed to the subject, gesturing and grinning, all the while bobbing his head. "Ye'd be able to stay in the Highlands, lass, and ye—"

"Nae," she blurted. Determination and boldness bolted through her, and she notched her chin upward. "Nae," she repeated, raising her voice to make sure he heard her correctly. "I won't."

Chapter Fifteen

COBURN LONGED TO lift Fleming and shake him like the vermin he was, the wee sneaky rat. Only Logan's slight head shake prevented him from giving in to the reckless urge.

Her anger palpable, Arieen shook her head, livid shards shining in her eyes.

"I absolutely cannot believe you." She made a brusque gesture with her hand. "This visit wasn't about me or my forgiveness, but about you and your selfish aspirations."

No wonder he'd been agreeable about giving Arieen her belongings, and why he'd insisted on following Coburn to Lockelieth.

"Why am I not surprised? You've wasted your time." She threw her hands into the air, evidently overcome with disgust. "Go home to your sons and wife. I'm staying here."

Fleming made a dismissive gesture, calculation gleaming in his emotionless eyes. "Ye dinna understand. His Grace has the connections to have me appointed a Scottish Laird of Parliament."

Coburn set his jaw against the curses tapping the back of his teeth.

"I'd be the equivalent of an English baron." Fleming extended his palms, his sycophant smile curdling Coburn's hastily gulped midday meal.

"Nae." Unyielding. Final.

The icy Arieen had returned.

"But, Arieen, the Duke of Strathorn will only petition the king on my behalf if ye agree to be his duchess." In his eagerness, Fleming edged closer. "Think, lass, what this means for ye."

Coburn eyed him with the same distaste he would an adder about to strike.

If he dared to touch her...

"Ye, the Duchess of Strathorn," Fleming said, his expression animated.

Logan made a disgusted noise in the back of his throat.

"Strathorn?" Such revulsion rippled through Coburn as he plunked his fists on his hips. "That sod?"

Pray tell, how was Strathorn in a position to aid Fleming in acquiring a barony? The duke was probably lying out his arse in order to marry Arieen.

How could Fleming consider such a union or contemplate subjecting her to that cur? Because Robert Fleming, the unmitigated self-serving sot, didn't give a tinker's damn about her.

She lifted a shoulder, raking him with a deprecating gaze. "I don't want to be a duchess, nor do I covet another title. I never have. I prefer a simpler life."

Her gaze met Coburn's, and he read in her eyes what he'd dared not dream.

She wanted to marry *him*.

Not a duke or a viscount or any other man holding a title. No lofty-positioned nob, but him, a humble Scot. If his heart battered his ribs harder, they'd be bruised, and everyone present would hear the jubilant drumbeat.

Fleming's whole demeanor changed, and he advanced, stalking toward her. "I'm legally yer guardian, Arieen."

"You publicly renounced me."

She didn't flinch but thrust her chin out and pointing at him, proudly challenged him.

"Aye, I did, and I regret I allowed my anger to speak." His countenance grew flinty. The ruthless businessman had emerged. "In the eyes of the courts, ye are my daughter, and I can force ye."

He was right, damn him to Hades.

That settled Coburn's mind. He'd nae allow Fleming to take her away from him. They'd exchange vows today. And consummate the marriage. There could be no waiting as she'd asked.

Her smile blinding, she crossed the room to stand next to him. "Not if I'm already married. I've accepted Coburn's offer."

Not caring who looked on, he tucked her to his side and took her hand. "Aye, and I'm honored above all men."

"No' all," came Logan's glib reply as he mimicked his cousin's posture and drew Mayra near.

No doubt seeing his scheme about to be thwarted, Fleming's face reddened, all pretense of civility fleeing. He pointed a finger and shook it. "Ye're underage. I forbid it."

"Logan?" Mayra raised on her toes and spoke softly into his ear.

He grinned and hugged her. "Aye, my love, that was my thought, too."

Coburn glanced down at Arieen, and spoke low for her ears alone. "I promise I shallna let him take ye from me."

She angled her neck to look at him. "I ken."

So simple. No argument, only blind faith in him. His heart welled that he should be so blessed to be loved by this remarkable woman.

The butler entered carrying fresh tea. "Sir, the reply ye awaited has arrived. Ye asked that I inform ye at once."

After exchanging the cooled teapot with the warm brew, he passed Logan a missive.

With a flick of his thumb, Logan broke the wax and quickly perused the contents. "Excellent." Logan, looking entirely too pleased with himself, handed the note to Coburn. "Please ask Mrs. Granger and Mrs. McIntyre to join us."

That caused the bland-faced butler's jowls to jiggle and his brows to twitch. "Aye, sir."

Coburn perused the short reply and, checking a triumphant arcing of his mouth, refolded the paper and slid it inside his coat pocket.

"Come, let's have a seat and enjoy the hot tea, shall we?" Logan motioned toward the table. "I'm sure we can come to an agreement over Mrs. McIntyre's delicious dainties."

Coburn sent him a quizzical glance.

Logan winked.

What the hell was he doing? Why offer Fleming tea? He'd rather boot his sorry arse to the door and send for the priest. Still, Coburn guided Arieen to the sofa and they sat.

Fleming grudgingly took a seat as well. "I'm no' leavin' without Arieen. I have the law on my side."

"And you think to force me to go with you?" She quirked a brow. "By yourself?"

"She's stayin' and becomin' my wife." Coburn took her hand, and his heart tripped over itself at the sweet smile she gifted him. Why, she gazed at him in the same manner Mayra looked at Logan.

With adoration.

In the three days he'd been gone, he'd come to a startling realization.

He'd move the Highland's moors and mountains to make Arieen his wife. He finally understood Logan's desperation to win Mayra. Once you met your other half, how could you endure the rest of your life without her?

Inconceivable.

He loved Arieen beyond logic.

Acting the perfect hostess, Mayra poured everyone tea. She'd passed the last cup to Coburn, when the trio of servants filed in.

Eyes wide and curious, they exchanged glances, then gazed at each of the room's occupants in turn.

"Thank ye. Please stand there." Logan pointed to behind Coburn and Arieen.

Without hesitation, they did as he directed.

"Cousin, what are ye doin'?" Coburn asked.

"What a laird does for his clan. Protectin' his people." Logan set his cup aside and inhaled, his chest expanding with the gusty breath.

Arieen gave Coburn a confused look, but he raised a brow. "I dinna have a clue, lass."

"Coburn, ye love Arieen, dinna ye? And ye'd forsake all others for her, wouldna ye?" Logan leaned forward, his elbows on his knees.

"Aye, I do love her, and I have forsaken all others." Coburn peered into her eyes, brimming with love for him and took her hand. "I'll cherish ye until I draw my last breath."

The radiant smile she bestowed upon him would've rendered hell's deepest pit midday bright.

"And ye willin'ly take her to wife until the good Laird calls ye home?" Logan asked.

His heartbeat quickened as raw emotion stimulated the organ. "Aye willin'ly, humbly, and gratefully, if she'll have me."

"And Arieen," Mayra said as Logan clasped her hand. "Ye love Coburn and are willin' to take him to husband for the rest of yer days?"

"Aye, I do, and I am." Giving Coburn an endearing sideways smile, Arieen met Fleming's glower. "Just as soon as a man of God is willing to perform the ceremony."

His scowl growing darker, Fleming made a dismissive sound and gesture.

"So ye think ye love each other. It's of nae importance. Marriages are no' about sentimental drivel. They are arranged for position—social and financial gain. If ye must, become lovers after ye wed Strathorn. For marry him ye will, Arieen."

Logan stood, looking every bit the Laird of Lockelieth. "That's nae possible, Flemin'. Under Scotland's irregular marriage laws, a couple professin' their willingness to become man and wife in front of witnesses is a legally bindin' union."

Arieen inhaled sharply, and eyes wide, swiveled toward Coburn. "Did you know what he was about?"

"I suspected what he intended." He ran his gaze over her face, wishing it could be his fingers. "Do ye object?"

Humor softened her features, and she chuckled. "Nae, I don't. I was surprised, that's all. I don't know anyone who wasn't married in a proper church ceremony." She leaned into him. "'Tis fitting, I think. We've not gone about courtship and wedding in the normal fashion. Why start now?"

"Nae. I willna let the matter go." Fleming lurched to his feet. "Arieen is my property to do with as I wish. This farce canna be defended in court."

"Aye, it can. Even when no cleric is present, Coburn and Arieen are married. There are five witnesses besides ye to attest to it." Logan canted his head toward the servants.

"Verra well done, my laird." Mrs. Granger said, eyeing Robert with the same contempt she would vermin in the larder.

Beaming, Brewster and Mrs. McIntyre bobbed their heads in agreement.

Nostrils flared, Fleming sneered, "I'll have the union annulled."

"That could take years, Robert," Arieen said with more patience than Coburn possessed. "No one, not even your duke, will wait that long to marry me."

"Besides," Coburn said, "Arieen and I well might have children by then. Nae annulment will be granted if we do." He'd do his best to make sure they did. "Ye need to concede defeat."

"Nae." His face *riddy* and brow damp, Fleming appeared on the verge of an apoplexy, yet he obstinately shook his head.

Coburn stood and drew Arieen to her feet. He patted his pocket. "The note just delivered was a reply from the minister. He'll be here within the hour to perform a ceremony that will consecrate our nuptials in the eyes of the church."

Fleming was beaten.

Logan angled his head toward Brewster. "Please escort Mr. Flemin' to the door."

Fleming stamped to the doorway. He scraped a critical gaze over the salon. "Ye could've lived in one of Scotland's grandest houses, Arieen. Yet, ye choose to live in this crumblin' piece of shite. I am well done with ye."

Pompous wee prig of a mon.

With another snarl, he clomped from the room, followed by the servants.

"I'd like a few minutes with Arieen before the minister arrives." Coburn touched her elbow.

Despite her valiance, white lines bracketed her mouth.

"Of course." Logan led Mayra from the salon but, at the door, she sent Arieen a reassuring smile.

Hands on her shoulders, Coburn rotated her until they stood face to face. "Are ye all right?"

"Aye. I shan't let Robert's disappointment and hatred ruin the most wonderful day of my life." Her lips trembled the merest bit. "Do ye truly love me, Coburn Wallace? As much as I adore ye?"

He pulled her tight to him and buried his face in her neck.

"Aye, aye, my sweet lass, I do. More than the heather blossoms on the moors. I love ye with a fiery ache that grows each passin' day. I dinna deserve ye, but I shall spend each hour of my life grateful ye'd have a mon like me."

"And I love you, Coburn." She entwined her arms around his neck, running her fingers through his hair as she angled her face to meet his lips. "When did you say the minister was arriving?"

"At any moment." He kissed the corner of her mouth, then darted his tongue out to taste its nectar. "Ye dinna believe Logan, that we're married under Scottish irregular marriage laws?"

Arieen smiled and shook her head. "Nae, I believe him."

"Ye want to make sure Flemin' canna have the union annulled?"

Over Coburn's dead body.

"Nae. That's not why I asked." She brushed her lips across his jaw, and the heat in his blood sent desire pulsing to every inch of his body. "I'm wondering how long I have to wait to approach the man I love about consummating our union."

If he didn't fear they'd be interrupted, he'd do so right here.

"Ye may no' have to wait a verra long time after all." She gave him a coy look, and he barely suppressed a groan.

He eyed the sofa assessing its length. Nae. Not their first time. He wanted their joining to be a powerful, sensual memory they carried with them the rest of their lives.

He grinned and kissed her nose. "An eager lass, are ye?"

"Coburn, I've wanted you since you made my knees go weak when you kissed me at the ball."

He searched her face, loving this woman more than he'd ever believed himself capable of. "Nae regrets, Arieen? 'Tis no' too late—"

"*Shh.*" She touched two fingers to his lips. "No regrets, my dearest love. Not now. Not ever."

EPILOGUE

Lockelieth Keep, Scottish Highlands
1 September 1720

ARIEEN HUMMED A Scottish ballad as she pulled the drapery aside to peer at the drive again. She released the fabric and as it settled back into place, resumed pacing. Today, she'd meet Captain Donal MacDuff, the half-Scots, half-English ship's captain claiming to be her real father.

She fingered the ruby brooch at her neckline as she wore a nervous path into the carpet.

In his last letter, Captain MacDuff had specifically asked her to wear the gem. He vowed the brooch was confirmation—at least in his mind—she was, indeed, his daughter.

It seemed, she had two sisters and two brothers. It had been one of her brothers who'd spotted her at McCullough's masquerade ball. Because of her strong resemblance to his sisters, he knew at once she must be a relation. That explained his shocked and intrigued expression.

Her four older siblings were also coming today.

Arieen's stomach fluttered, and she pressed a hand to the tension thrumming there. Here she had thought she had no brothers and sisters, and instead, she had two of each.

If she was Donal MacDuff's daughter.

Coburn took her hand and gave her fingers a light squeeze.

"Are ye nervous, *leannan*?"

"A mite"—*a lot*—"but in a pleasant sort of way."

She brushed her gloved hand over the skirt of her new rose and gold *robe à la française* gown. Silly of her, but she'd wanted to impress the man claiming to be her father. This man who wanted her to be his daughter, despite the circumstances of her birth.

How very different than Robert Fleming.

Her beloved husband appeared every bit the proper gentleman today as well.

How she adored the handsome rogue.

Coburn had eschewed his normal attire, and wore a midnight blue frock coat and matching breeches. Why, he'd even conceded to wear a lace jabot tied about his neck. A rare concession, indeed. Except for gingerish hair, no one would've taken him for a Highlander.

"Coburn, do you think I really am Captain MacDuff's daughter?" she asked, unable to keep the anxiety from her voice.

Until a month ago, she assumed she'd never know anything about her real father. The captain had been at sea when his son had seen her at the ball. He'd had to wait weeks until Captain MacDuff returned to England to tell his father he'd discovered Arieen. Or so the captain's first correspondence claimed.

"I dinna ken, but he'd be lucky if ye are." Coburn led her to the sofa. "Sit down, lass. Yer pacin' is makin' *me* nervous."

"What if he's mistaken?" Biting her lower lip, she sank onto the cushion. She'd refused to harbor false hope. Soon enough, the truth would out.

Coburn also sat and, draping an arm about her shoulders, kissed her temple. "Dinna fash yerself. He must be pretty confident he's yer father. If he isna, ye'll still always have me and Logan and Mayra."

She rested her head on his shoulder, entwining her fingers with his. She'd grown impossibly more in love with him these past months. The more time they spent together, the more she admired and respected him.

"I know, Coburn, and I count my blessings every day that you came into my life." One fateful night at a masquerade ball and the course of both of their lives had changed forever. "You rescued me just like a romantic legendary hero."

"Nae, ye rescued *me*." He tipped her chin upward, and her gaze sank to his mouth. That mouth that had so enticed her that fateful night.

"No man has loved a woman as much as I love ye, Arieen Wallace."

"Although it galls me, I think I must be grateful to Robert. If he hadn't cast me out, you'd not have felt the need to rush to save me. We mightn't have had a chance to love like this." She sighed and snuggled into his side.

Coburn made a growling sound in his throat. "I canna think kindly on him. He'd have bartered ye like a prize horse or sow to get what he wanted, the craven."

"A horse or sow?" she asked incredulously while sitting straight and giving his arm a playful slap. "You are no poet, Coburn Lain Calan Wallace."

"I beg yer pardon, lass." Releasing a melodious chuckle, Coburn kissed her nose. "I meant it in the most flatterin' way."

Brewster stepped inside the doorframe. "Yer guests have arrived, Mr. and Mrs. Wallace."

Arieen's tummy went all warm and melty. How she loved being called Mrs. Wallace. Taking a bracing breath, she stood.

Coburn did as well before tucking her hand into the crook of his elbow.

He'd scarcely finished giving her an encouraging smile when Donal MacDuff and his striking sons and daughters entered the salon.

One look and Coburn whistled. "By Odin. The resemblance is uncanny. Ye are kin for certain."

Arieen gazed into two pairs of eyes much like hers, then smiled as she recognized the man from the ball who'd regarded her with such acute interest.

A pleasant chaos reigned for several minutes as introductions, amidst hugs, smiles and tears were managed. Her brothers were Leslie and Glen, and her sisters Arable and Donella. Leslie was the eldest at nine-and-twenty and Donella the youngest at one-and-twenty. All except Donella were married and had children.

Finally, when everyone had calmed and they sat sipping tea and enjoying Mrs. McIntyre's delicious shortbread and scones, Captain MacDuff pointed at Arieen's ruby pin.

"May I see it, please, Arieen?"

She opened the clasp then handed the brooch to him.

"I gave this to Osla as a token of my love. My substitute for a Luckenbooth brooch." A melancholic smile bent his lips as he turned it over. "See the inscription here, Arieen?"

He pointed to the backside of the doves.

She squinted, unable to make out what he pointed out. "I'm sorry, but without my spectacles, I cannot read small writing."

The captain chuckled and patted her hand. "Neither could your mother, but she refused to wear her spectacles. Said they made her look old."

Coburn leaned in and peered at the jewel.

"A 'D' is engraved on one dove," he said, "and an 'O' on the other." He gave Arieen a heartening, closed-lip smile.

"I was a widower." A far off look in his eyes, the captain brushed his callused thumb over the silver doves. "I didn't think to marry again until I met your mother at a house party given by my elder brother. I asked for her hand on four occasions, and the Earl of Lennox refused me each time. A lowly sea captain wasn't respectable enough, you see."

So, her grandfather had been an earl.

In all these years, he'd never made any attempt to contact Arieen.

Captain MacDuff gazed into the distance, sadness etched on his wind-weathered face. "I didn't know she was with child when I sailed. The ship foundered, and a year passed before I limped home. I sought Osla straightaway, but all Lennox would tell me was that she'd fallen in love and married in my absence."

"She *never* loved Robert Fleming." Even as a child, Arieen had recognized that brutal truth.

He patted Arieen's hand again, his eyes watery. "I didn't know about you, Arieen. Please believe me."

"I do," she said, her heart swelling with happiness.

They visited for a short while longer, then her family took their leave amid promises to invite Arieen and Coburn to visit soon.

Once they'd gone, she wrapped her arms around Coburn's waist. She held him tight and tilted her head to meet his loving gaze.

"I'm glad to know I have a family, but if I didn't, I want you to know you are all I'll ever need. I never knew what contentment was until I married you."

"And ye are everythin' my heart has ever desired." He winked and lowered his head. "I'm verra glad ye stole a kiss from me, my pirate lass."

"Aye, and I'm very glad you let me."

She eyed the drawing room door, then giving into naughty whimsy, crossed the room and locked the door. An invitation in her gaze, she clasped his hand and drew him to the sofa.

Coburn cocked a brow even as a seductive grin swept his face. "The servants will gossip."

"*Hmph*, as if they don't now already." She placed his hand on her breast, arching into his firm caress. "It was you who desired to practice bedsport in the library window seat two weeks ago. I swear someone walked in on us."

"Only *one* with all of yer moanin'?"

His feigned shock earned him a swat on the buttocks. "Rogue."

He traced the seam of her mouth with his tongue, and growled, "Let me taste yer mouth, lass."

She parted her lips and, as always, the magic of their love swept her away.

About the Author

USA Today Bestselling, award-winning author COLLETTE CAMERON pens Scottish and Regency historicals, featuring rogues, rapscallions, rakes, and the intelligent, intrepid damsels who reform them.

Blessed with fantastic fans as well as a compulsive, overactive, and witty Muse who won't stop whispering new romantic romps in her ear, she lives in Oregon with her mini-dachshunds, though she dreams of living in Scotland part-time. You'll always find dogs, birds, occasionally naughty humor, and a dash of inspiration in her sweet-to-spicy timeless romances®.

Her motto for life? You can't have too much chocolate, too many hugs, too many flowers, or too many books. She's thinking about adding shoes to that list.

Connect with Collette!

www.collettecameron.com
Newsletter: signup.collettecameron.com/theregencyrose
Facebook.com/collettecameronauthor
Bookbub.com/authors/collette-cameron
Instagram.com/collettecameronauthor
Twitter @Collette_Author
Pinterest.com/colletteauthor

Made in the USA
Lexington, KY
10 December 2019

58364753R00083